KB148210

박윤주, 찰스윤의

스토리가 있는 영어 II

박윤주 · 찰스윤 공저

에피스테메
EPISTEME

박윤주 · 찰스윤의
스토리가 있는 영어 II

저자 / 박윤주 · 찰스윤
발행인 / 조남철
발행처 / 한국방송통신대학교출판부
주소 / 서울특별시 종로구 이화동 57번지 (110-500)
전화 / 1644-1232
FAX / (02)741-4570
http://press.knou.ac.kr
출판등록 / 1982. 6. 7. 제1-491호
초판 1쇄 발행 / 2011. 2. 21.

ⓒ 박윤주 · 찰스윤, 2011
ISBN 978-89-20-00579-4 93840
값 12,000원

편집 · 조판 / 하람커뮤니케이션
일러스트 / 박완기

■ 이 책의 내용에 대한 무단 복제 및 전재를 금하며 저자와 한국방송통신대학교출판부의
　허락 없이는 어떠한 방식으로든 2차적 저작물을 출판하거나 유포할 수 없습니다.

■ 잘못 만들어진 책은 바꾸어 드립니다.

두 번째 책으로 인사를 드리게 되서 매우 기쁩니다. 우리의 일상생활이 반영된 영어회화 교재 덕분에 힘을 얻으셨다는 분들이 너무 많으셨거든요. 그분들의 격려가 원동력이 되어, 1권의 주인공들과 더 많은 등장인물을 초대한 2권이 탄생하였습니다.

1권과 마찬가지로 범국가적인 등장인물들이 변화무쌍한 서울 생활을 겪는 이야기로 영어 회화를 풀어갑니다. 집 구하기나, 구직 등과 같은 실용적인 내용들이 있는가 하면, 애완동물에 대한 견해 차이나 한국생활에서의 다양성을 반영한 주제들로 엮은 2권은 한국에서 영어를 배우는 여러분들의 이야기이기 때문에 더욱 친근하게 느껴질 겁니다.

내용상의 특성을 살펴보면, 각 장은 Key Patterns, Alternative Expressions, Focus on Pronunciation, Real & Live, Exercises로 구성되어 있습니다. 우선 Key Patterns를 통해서 여러 분은 나를 중심으로 하는 발화 'I-Expression' 상대편의 대화를 이끌어내는 'You-Expression' 다양한 종류의 'Statements 평서문', 그리고 유용한 'Questions 의문문' 표현을 익히실 수 있습니다. 대화문의 문장 가운데에서 흥미로운 표현 5가지를 골라 엮은 Alternative Expressions는 여러분의 어휘와 문장 수준을 한 단계 높여줄 것입니다. "이런 한국어 표현은 어떻게 말하지?"라는 궁금증은 Real & Live를 통해 풀어보세요. 그리고 늘 언제나 재미있는 Exercises로 마무리 하시기 바랍니다. 주제별로 엮은 Culture Corner는 미국 문화에 대한 유익한 읽을거리, 생각할 거리를 제공할 것입니다.

두 번째 교재의 처음부터 끝까지 애써준 성지연 선생님 너무 고마워요. 이번에도 예쁜 그림으로 책을 꾸며준 박완기 선생님 감사합니다. 이 교재가 여러분을 또 한번 즐겁고 행복한 영어회화의 길로 안내하길 진심으로 바랍니다.

박윤주

For our second book on English conversation, the authors have once again attempted to select useful, practical expressions that capture the naturalness of English language in everyday use. As with the first book, Book II attempts to ground the key expressions and structures in a transnational context. Thus, the dialogues will hopefully resonate with our readers as they are located in the vibrant city of Seoul, a city which features an ever-growing population of foreigners who will continue to influence and shape the usage of English in this country.

Characters from the first book continue their roles in this work with a few additional characters. The themes and storylines presented here are still functional—asking for directions, searching for an apartment or applying for a job,—but also more psychological—cultural preferences for pets, diversity of experiences of expatriates living in South Korea, etc. Again, it is our sincere hope that students will find this book to be more challenging and engaging as they continue their personal journeys in studying English conversation.

In addition to the colleagues who reviewed this work, the authors owe a debt of gratitude to Jiyeon Sung for an outstanding job in helping us bring this book to completion.

Charse Yun

Contents

Scope and Sequence

Themes	Lessons	Key Patterns	Real & Live	Culture Notes
I Meeting the Sister	1 The Advice of Friends	• I'm worried that~ • You could start by~ • It's not as if~ • What would you do if~?	• 진짜 옷을 잘 입어, 멋쟁이야! • 그는 눈치가 빨라!	Weddings in the U.S.
	2 Alex and His Sister	• All I'm saying is that~ • You never really appreciate~ until~ • The important thing is~ • When do you expect to~?	• 모르는 척 하지 마! • 최고야!	
II Housing	3 Moving	• I've heard that~ • You do know~, don't you? • All I need is~ • Do you know where the best place is to~?	• 잠을 못 잤다고? • 왜 그렇게 힘들게 하는데?	Housing in the U.S.
	4 Checking the Place Out	• I wish I could~ • You might as well~ • That's a little on the~ side~ • What makes you~?	• 진짜 늦은 시간 • 계속해봐! 움직이라고!	
III Getting around Seoul	5 Lost in Itaewon	• I wonder~ • Would you happen to know~ • It would save (us) a lot of~ • Which way (is it)?	• 그렇게 되지 않았어. 불행이야. • 엎친 데 덮친 격이야	Getting Around Seoul
	6 ATM	• I was in the middle of~ • Do you mind if~ • Let's try to~ • Where can I~?	• 진짜 웃겨! • 진짜 비싸요.	
	7 International Clinic	• I understand that~ • You're better off~ • I'd be (more) worried about~ (than) • Since when did you~?	• 저는 모범생입니다. • 데이트에서 기초 중의 기초라고.	

IV Cats and Dogs	8 At Stella's Apartment	• I'd much rather~ • Are you~ or~? • This is such a~ • How did you manage to~?	• 가구 찾으러 여기저기 다녔어요. • 우리는 제법 잘 어울려요.	
	9 Korea and Cats	• I never would have taken~ • Once you get to know~ • They still haven't caught on~ • Why do you~?	• 나는 말짱해요. • 그는 술을 마시면 다 친구가 돼요.	Pets in the U.S.
	10 In Praise of Cats	• I've never (liked)~ • You'd be surprised~ • I'd still choose A over B. • What is it that makes~ so special?	• 밑져야 본전이라고, 잃을 것도 없잖아! • 난 네게 반했어.	
V Business Matters	11 Job Interview	• I used to~ • You were saying? • The position involves~ • Who gave you that idea~?	• 그는 원칙을 어기고 있어요. • "우리"를 중시한다고.	Resume and Interview Tips
	12 Business Meeting	• I have decided~ • You've got it all wrong~ • We'll miss out~ • What about~?	• 꽝이야! • 열두 시 반 정도에 만나뵙는 걸로 하지요.	
	13 Business Problem	• I don't see why not~ • Can you believe~? • We have no choice but to~ • Whatever happened to~?	• 모든 것을 걸었어요. • 전혀 말이 안 돼.	
VI Music and Words	14 Musical Director	• I imagine that~ • As long as you~ • A (a few things) go/es with B. • When is the latest~?	• 오늘은 이만 하지. • 저랑 천천히 단계를 밟으면, 할 수 있습니다.	The Changing Face of Korea
	15 Talk Show	• I really had no idea~ • You're in for~ • When it comes down to~ • What is it with~?	• 너는 너무 근시안이야. • 나는 편한 사람이에요.	

Characters

Soyeong Jennifer Michael

Alex Matthew Stella

Soyeong	A Korean student who works. She is interested in theater and is friends with Jennifer.
Jennifer	A friend of Soyeong' s from the U.S.
Michael	A newly arrived theater director from Canada
Alex	A Korean American who works in finance
Matthew	An American who is Jennifer' s boyfriend
Stella	A professor of English from Canada

Theme I

Meeting the Sister

Lesson 1

The Advice of Friends

Lesson 2

Alex and His Sister

In Theme I, Soyeong rushes in to tell her close friends Jennifer and Jane about some sudden news. Her boyfriend Alex's sister is unexpectedly visiting Seoul this weekend. Since Alex and his sister are very close, Soyeong is naturally nervous. To her dismay, Soyeong's friend Jane is only increasing her anxiety. Jennifer, on the other hand, tries to be more reassuring. The scene then switches to Alex and his sister. The dinner concluded, Alex and his sister Grace discuss how the evening went and his prospects of marriage to Soyeong. After some goading, Alex expresses no hurry to wed while his sister warns him that marriage should be taken more seriously.

The Advice of Friends

Soyeong   Hey guys! You'll never guess what just happened!

Jennifer   What? Tell me!

Soyeong   Alex's sister is unexpectedly making a surprise visit to Seoul, and I have to meet her for dinner this weekend!

Jennifer   Wow. So you're stressed out, huh?

Jane   What's the big deal? So you meet his sister. **It's not as if** you're meeting his parents or something.

Jennifer   You don't understand. Alex is really close with his older sister. He really looks up to her and respects her opinion more than anyone else's⋯ including his own parents!

Jane   Wow! That's worse than being a "Momma's Boy"! He's a "sister's boy"!

Soyeong   You're not helping! **What would you do if** you were in my shoes?

Jane   Okay, okay. I'm only teasing. But seriously, **what's the worst that could happen**?

Soyeong **I'm worried that** if I don't make a good first impression, everything could start off on the wrong foot.

Jennifer I wouldn't worry about that if I were you. Just relax and be yourself. I'm sure you two will hit it off.

Jane Yeah, no worries. Wear your heart on your sleeve. You have such a winning personality, I'm sure it will all turn out fine.

Soyoeng I guess I'm just a bit nervous. What I mean to say is that Alex cares so much for his sister's opinion. She's the main influence in his life. He listens to everything she says!

Jane Hmm, that doesn't sound right. Maybe he isn't the guy you want to be dating after all.

Soyeong Ugh, could you please knock it off? I really need your help!

Jennifer We're here for you, Soyeong. Tell us how we can help.

Soyeong **You could start by** telling me what I should wear!

Key Patterns

1. I'm worried that~   I'm worried about you.

2. You could start by~
   You could start by telling me what I should wear!

3. It's not as if~
   It's not as if you're meeting his parents or something.

4. What would you do if~?
   What would you do if you were in my shoes?

1

I'm worried that _____ _____ 할까 걱정이다.
I'm worried about you.

우선 be worried about/be worried that 구문으로 "어떤 일이나 상황에 대해서 걱정이 된다, ~할까 걱정이다"라는 뜻입니다.

A. be worried about + 명사/대명사: ~할까 걱정이다.

I'm worried about you a lot. 저는 당신이 많이 걱정돼요.
I'm really worried about the economic situation these days.
나는 요즘 경제 상황에 대해서 걱정이 됩니다.

B. be worried that + 절 (주어 + 동사)

I'm worried that the chairperson might get upset.
저는 의장님이 화를 낼까 봐 걱정이에요.
I'm worried that if I don't make a good first impression, everything could start off on the wrong foot.
나는 내가 좋은 첫인상을 남기지 않으면, 모든 일을 처음부터 다시 해야 할까 봐 걱정이라고.

2

You could start by _____ . _____로부터 시작하세요.
You could start by telling me what I should wear!

『영어회화 II』Key Patterns에서는 You Expression을 새롭게 시작합니다. 대화란 상호간의 의사소통이나, 'You and me', 즉 당신과 내가 존재하는 것이고, 상대편에 관련된 문장이 그만큼 풍부해야겠죠? You와 관련된 첫 번째 문장을 살펴봅니다. You could start by + 동사~ing입니다. "~로부터 시작하세요"라는 다소 우회적인 제안의 표현입니다.

A. You could start by + 동사 ~ing: ~로부터 시작하세요.

You could start by telling me what I should wear!
내가 무슨 옷을 입어야 하는지부터 말해줘!
> A: Do you really want to go on a diet?
> 정말 다이어트를 시작하시려고요?
> B: You could start by drinking lots of water and walking briskly.
> 물을 많이 마시고요, 빨리 걷기부터 시작하세요.

3

It's not as if _____ . _____와 같은 것은 아니잖아요.
It's not as if you're meeting his parents or something.

It's not as if~는 표현 그대로, "~와 같은 것은 아니잖아요"입니다. 최소한 어느 정도는 된다는, 그러므로 최악의 상황은 피했다는 느낌을 담고 있습니다.

A. It's not as if + 주어 + 동사: ~와 같은 것은 아니잖아요.

It's not as if you're meeting his parents or something.
네가 그의 부모님을 만나거나 뭐 그런 상황은 아니잖아.

It's not as if you're in charge of everything.

당신이 모든 것을 책임져야 하는 것은 아니지 않습니까.

4

What would you do if _____?

만일 _____ 라면 어떻게 하시겠습니까?

What would you do if you were in my shoes?

What would you do if~는 아주 자주 사용하실 수 있는 유용한 구문입니다. 상대방에게 if 다음 문장에 대해서, "만약 ~라면 어떻게 하시겠습니까?"라고 묻는 형태이거든요. 이 구문은 if 절을 공부할 때 가장 기본적으로 익히는 문장입니다. 우회적으로 자신의 의견을 피력할 수 있는 표현이 될 수 있으니 자신의 표현이 될 때까지 끊임없이 연습하세요.

A. What would you do if + 주어 + 동사: 만약 ~라면 어떻게 하시겠습니까?

What would you do if you were in my shoes?

당신이 제 상황이라면 어떻게 하시겠습니까?
– 위의 문장에서는 'be in one's shoes',
즉 "다른 누군가의 구두를 신었다"는 표
현이 '다른 상황에 처한 타인의 입장이
되다'라는 의역이 된다는 것도 같이 익
히시기 바랍니다.

What would you do if you had only a month to live?

당신 생명이 만약 딱 한 달 남았다면 어떻게
하실래요?

Alternative Expressions

1

You'll never guess what just happened!

= Wait till you hear this!

= Boy, do I have news for you!

= You won't believe this!

= You're not going to believe this, but~

= Get a load of this!

= Check this out!

2

Stressed out

= freaking out

= going crazy

= losing one's mind

3

What's the worst that could happen?

= What's the worst-case scenario?

= How much worse can it get?

= [It] can't get much worse.

= If worst comes to worst~

Also:

got the worst of it~

That's the worst of it.

4

Start off on the right/wrong foot

Positive:

= hit it off well.

= make a good first impression.

Negative:

= We had a bumpy start.

= We had a rocky start.

= We didn't hit it off.

= Could we restart?

= Could we start over again?

= Let's make a fresh start.

5

Wear your heart on your sleeve

"heart on sleeve" means to express emotions freely

Related expressions with the word "heart":

He/She is all heart

He/She is a sweetheart.

He/She has a heart of gold.

heart is/isn't in the right place

Real & Live

Real and Live는 한국어와 영어 모두 생생하게 살아 움직이는 표현을 배우는 장입니다.
여러분들 잘 알고 계시겠죠?

1. 진짜 옷을 잘 입어, 멋쟁이야! He/She is a sharp dresser.

한동안 얼짱, 몸짱, 센스짱 등 뭔가 뛰어난 부분에 대해서 "~짱"이라는 표현을 많이 사
용했었습니다. 패셔니스타나 스타일이라는 영어표현도 한국어 대화 중에 많이 사용되었
고요. 영어로 간단하게 표현하면 어떨까요? 4가지 다 유용하게 사용하실 수 있는 표현
이고, 특히 sharp dresser라는 말은 정말 edge가 살아 있지요?·

- He/She is a good/fantastic dresser.
- He/She knows clothes well.
- He/She is very fashionable.

2. 그는 눈치가 진짜 빨라! He reads people well.

눈치에 대한 표현을 여러 가지로 살펴봅니다. 우선 눈치를 챈다는 것은 상대편의 기분이나 감정, 상황을 굉장히 빠른 시간에 알아낸다는 것이죠? read를 일반적으로 책을 읽는다고만 이해하시는 분들! "그는 내 마음을 잘 읽어낸다"는 것은 무슨 뜻일까요? 그렇죠. 역시 눈치가 빠르시군요.

눈치가 없는 경우라면 clueless, 말 그대로 실마리가 없다는 표현을 사용하고, 티 나는 모습을 잘 알아차린다면 '알게 되다, 이해하다' 는 뜻의 tell을 적절하게 사용하십시오. 참 쉽죠?

A: 그녀는 사람들 마음을 잘 알아. She reads people well.
B: 그 남자 진짜 눈치가 없다. He's clueless.
C: 그 사람 피곤한 티가 난다. I can tell he's tired.

Alex and His Sister

Grace   I had a great time. Dinner was wonderful.

Alex   I'm glad you finally had a chance to meet Soyeong. Isn't she great?

Grace   She seems so nice. And I really loved her dress! She has a good eye for fashion.

Alex   Yes, she certainly has good taste in things like clothing and food. But what did you think of her personality?

Grace   What's not to like? She's quite introverted. You, on the other hand, are quite the social butterfly. I think she would be really good for you. You really ought to do your best to make sure this one doesn't get away!

Alex   I thought you might say something like that. I guess I talk about you so much to Soyeong that she was a bit nervous to meet you. She knows how much I care about what you think!

Grace   Alex! You shouldn't have done that! You know I trust your judgment! Anyways, it doesn't matter what I think. **The important thing is** what you think.

Alex　Haha. I know. **All I'm saying is** that it's really important to me that you had a chance to meet her. I just want the two of you to get along.

Grace　Of course we will. Why wouldn't we? You're being silly. But there's something I really want to ask you. **When do you expect to tell Mom and Dad the big news?**

Alex　Hmmm⋯ What do you mean?

Grace　Stop playing dumb! You know what I mean! The wedding!

Alex　Haha. I have no idea what you're talking about. It's still too early, don't you think?

Grace　Come on. Are you saying that you guys haven't talked about marriage yet? You've been pretty serious for the past six months. The topic must have come up at least once! ✏

Alex　Hey! Cut me some slack, will you? There's plenty of time. Mom and Dad will visit Seoul next month. We'll talk about it then.

Grace　Whatever you say, little brother. The important thing to remember is that women can't wait forever. I'd check out some rings if I were you! **You never really appreciate** something until it's gone!

Key Patterns

1. All I'm saying is that~
   All I'm saying is that it's really important to me that you had a chance to meet her.

2. You never really appreciate~ until~
   You never really appreciate something until it's gone!

3. The important thing is~
   The important thing is what you think.

4. When do you expect to~?
   When do you expect to tell Mom and Dad the big news?

1

All I'm saying is that _____. 제가 말하고자 하는 바는 _____.
All I'm saying is that it's really important to me that you had a chance to meet her.

All I'm saying is that~ 구문입니다. 이미 했던 말을 다시 정리하거나, 부연 설명하고자 할 때 주위를 환기시키는 표현이라고 생각하세요. All I'm saying is that~ "제가 말하고자 하는 바는~"이라고 기억하시고, that 절 다음에 하고 싶은 문장을 말합니다. 특히, All이라는 단어 덕분에 본인의 의도라는 점, "오로지, 모든" 등의 뜻이 강화됩니다.

A. 본인의 뜻을 정확히 전달하고자 하는 All I'm saying is that~: 제가 말하고자 하는 바는~

All I'm saying is that it's really important to me that you had a chance to meet her.
내가 말하고자 하는 바는, 누나가(당신이) 그녀를 만나는 기회를 갖는 것이 내게 아주 중요하다는 거야.

B. 요점을 전달하고자 하는 All I'm saying is that~: All 대신에 what을 넣어서 표현할 수도 있습니다.

> A: I don't see your point. What do you mean by that?
> 무슨 얘기를 하는지 잘 이해를 못하겠어요. 그래서 뭐라고요?
>
> B: Um… what I'm saying is that I owe you a lot.
> 글쎄, 제가 말씀드리고자 하는 바는 제가 당신에게 많은 것을 빚지고 있다는 것입니다.

C. Are you saying that you guys haven't talked about marriage yet? 처럼 본문에서 나온 문장을 통해서 더 자세히 살펴볼까요? "너희 둘은 결혼에 대해서 얘기를 해본 적이 없다는 걸 말하고 싶은 거니?"라는 뜻입니다. "Are you telling me that~?", "Do you mean that~?", "Do you expect me to believe that~?" 등으로 다양하게 말할 수 있는데, 결국 주의를 집중시켜서 다시 한 번 확인하는 과정의 표현이라고 할 수 있겠죠.

2

You never really appreciate _____ until _____.
_____ 할 때까지 그 가치나 상황을 감사하지 못하다.
You never really appreciate something until it's gone!

You never really know/appreciate/think~ until~은 "~할 때까지 그 가치나 상황을 이해/감사/생각하지 못한다"는 구문입니다. You never really 다음에 뜻이 적합한 동사, 즉 상황에 따라 know, appreciate, think를 넣으세요. 그리고 until 다음에 주어 + 동사 절을 만듭니다.

A. You never really know~ until + 주어 + 동사: ~할 때까지 알지 못한다.

You never really appreciate something until it's gone!
당신은 중요한 것이 사라지고 난 후까지 그 가치를 이해하지 못할 거예요!
He never really knew what went wrong until she had left.
그는 그녀가 떠나갈 때까지 무엇이 잘못되었는지 알지 못했어요.

16

3

The important thing is _____.　중요한 것은 _____이다.
The important thing is what you think.

The important thing is~ 구문 역시 첫 번째 expression의 내용과 비슷하게, 중요한 내용을 다시 한 번 확인하고, 강조하는 구문이라고 할 수 있겠습니다. The important thing is~ + 접속사 + 주어 + 동사 절을 사용할 수도 있고, The important thing to + 동사 + Be 동사 + that 절로도 가능합니다.

A. The important thing is + 접속사 + 주어 + 동사: 중요한 것은~

The important thing is what you think.
중요한 것은 당신이 어떻게 생각하는가 하는 것입니다.

B. The important thing to + 동사 + Be 동사 + 접속사 + 주어 + 동사: ~해야 할 중요한 것은 ~입니다.

The important thing to remember is that women can't wait forever. 기억해야 할 정말 중요한 사실은 여자들은 결코 영원히 기다려주지 않는다는 점이야.

C. The only thing I know is~: 유일한 ~는~이다.

The only thing I know is that I love you.
유일한 사실은 내가 당신을 사랑한다는 겁니다.
The only way to get out of this poverty is to write a book.
지금 이 가난에서 벗어날 수 있는 유일한 방법은 책을 쓰는 것이다.

When do you expect to _____?

당신 생각에는 언제쯤 _____ 할 것 같아요?

When do you expect to tell Mom and Dad the big news?

When do you expect to~는 시간에 관한 가장 간단하면서도 유용한 표현입니다. "당신 생각에는 언제쯤 ~할 것 같아요?"라는 구문이에요.

A. When do you expect to + 동사: 언제 ~할 것 같아요?

When do you expect to tell Mom and Dad the big news?
너는 언제쯤 어머니와 아버지께 이 뉴스를 알릴 예정이니?

When do you expect to go back to your home country?
당신은 언제쯤 고국으로 돌아가실 예정입니까?

When do you expect to finish your work?
언제쯤 일이 끝날까요?

Alternative Expressions

1

I'm glad~

= I'm relieved to know~

= It's good to know that~

= It's nice to know that~

2

She has a good eye for~

= She has good taste.

= She has a sharp eye for~

= She knows how to pick them.

= She knows~ (e.g. "Bo knows baseball.")

= She really knows her stuff.

3

I thought you might say something like that.

= I figured you would say/do that.

= I guessed that would happen.

= I thought so.

= I thought that's what would happen.

= I knew you were going to say that.

4

Come on.

= Get real!   = Give me a break!

= Stop pulling my leg!   = Who are you kidding?

= Stop kidding around.   = You're fooling no one.

5

Are you saying that ～
= Are you telling me that～?
= Do you mean to say that～?
= What are you saying?
= Do you mean that～?
= Are you talking about～?
= Do you expect me to believe that～?

6

Cut me some slack!
= Give me a break!　　　= Ease off!
= Take it easy!　　　　 = Lay off, will you?

7

Whatever you say
= Yeah, right!　　　　 = Whatever!
= Hmph!

8

check out some rings
= To propose
= Ask for her/one's hand in marriage
= To pop the big question
= To go down on one knee
　 (and ask for one's hand)
= To walk down the aisle
= Wedding bells are ringing

1. 모르는 척 하지 마! Stop playing dumb!

의외로 까다로운 표현입니다. 혹시 '바보처럼 굴지 마'로 해석하신 건 아닌지요? 이미 다 알고 있으면서 모르는 척하는 상대편으로 인해 상처를 받는 경우가 간혹 있지요. 그럴 때 적절하게 사용하는 겁니다. "내가 바보인 줄 아는가 본데, 너야말로 그렇게 모르쇠를 잡지 말고, 정정당당하게 밝혀"라는 느낌을 확실히 주세요.

- 모르는 척 하지 마! Stop pretending you don't know!
- 모르는 것처럼 굴지 마! Stop acting like you don't know!
- 연기 그만하지! Drop the act!
- 사실대로 해! Be real with me!
- 흉내내지 말고! Quit faking!

2. 최고야! best bet!

Bet은 원래 내기, 혹은 내기를 건 물건이나 대상을 뜻합니다. 최고의 내기란 결국 이기는 것이고, 이긴다는 것은 최고의 상태를 선택하는 것입니다. 말 그대로 best choice 혹은 best option이라는 뜻이지요.

- NYU is your best bet, especially for a film major student like you.
  뉴욕대학교가 최선의 선택이야, 특히 너와 같은 영화 전공 학생에게는 말이지.
- 고려할 가치가 있는 것이야. Something you might want to look into.
  - i. You might want to check out.
  - ii. Something to look into
  - iii. It's worth looking.

Exercises

• Select the Appropriate Word

1. She's _____ introverted.
   a. well   b. quite

2. I guess I am _____ a bit nervous.
   a. just   b. only

3. You'll _____ guess what just happened!
   a. be   b. never

4. I thought you _____ say something like that.
   a. might   b. ought

5. Alex's sister is _____ coming to visit Seoul.
   a. unexpectedly   b. expectantly

6. You never really appreciate something _____ it's gone.
   a. up to   b. until

7. The important thing to _____ is that women can't wait forever.
   a. memory   b. remember

Culture Corner

• Weddings in the U.S.

In America, a number of interesting traditions have made their way into American weddings. In this article, we will look at a few of the major traditions and events in an American wedding.

The Proposal

Traditionally, the man proposes on bended knee to the woman and asks, "Will you marry me?" or "Will you be my wife?" To this day, many American men still perform the classical ritual of going down on one knee before their beloved to **ask for her hand in marriage**. Some men even ask their girlfriend's father for permission first, but this is not as common. It is considered rare for a woman to propose first. The most important thing about the proposal is the **engagement ring**. Typically, a man is said to save two months' wages to buy a diamond ring which the woman, if she accepts, will wear on the fourth finger of her left hand (known as the "**ring finger**"). Often, a man will buy the ring in secret and then "pop the question." Once she accepts, the couple is officially **engaged** and may now refer to each other as one's "**fiance**" (the man) and "**fiancée**" (the woman).

At the wedding itself, the man who is going to marry is known as "the **groom**" and the woman is known as "the **bride**." The groom's best or closest friend is called the "**best man**." For the bride, her best friend is "**the maid of honor**" or "**matron of honor**." The best man and matron of honor have important responsibilities in assisting the wedding ceremony and making sure that the reception goes well. The best man also traditionally organizes the **bachelor's party**, a celebration of the fiance's final days of male singlehood that usually involves much drinking and other raucous activities. It is limited to the groom's friends only. The maid of honor traditionally organizes the **bridal shower** which is limited to the female friends of the bride who give gifts. Sometimes the bride holds her own **bachelorette's party** where no men are allowed!

Gift Registry

In America these days, it is quite common for the couple to send out wedding invitations months in advance of the wedding date with a **gift registry**. That is, guests can look up the couple's name on an electronic list at a popular store and find a wish list of gifts that the couple has already pre-selected. It is expected that guests will purchase these wedding presents to help the new couple "start off" in their new life together. Thus, the gifts often take the form of appliances, furniture, china, silverware and other domestic household items.

The Marriage Ceremony

Many weddings are traditionally held at churches, but the locations can be quite diverse. Members of both the bride and groom's family will sit on the side of their respective parties. The ceremony is usually performed by a religious official such as a pastor or a priest, but marriages can also be performed by legal officials such as a justice of the peace. Each state has different laws regarding who can legally perform a marriage ceremony.

The term "**walk down the aisle**" refers to the long runway that leads to the place where the couple will exchange solemn vows. First, the groom, dressed in a tuxedo, will walk to the altar. He is followed by the **wedding party** consisting of various **groomsmen** and **bridesmaids**, including the maid of honor and the best man, also dressed in matching tuxedos and dresses. Small children also play the role of **ring boy** (carrying the wedding rings) and **flower girl**.

Finally, the pianist or organist will then strike the opening chords of the well-known "**The Bridal Chorus**" by Richard Wagner, signaling that the bride will begin her **processional**, or entrance. She is accompanied down the aisle by **the father of the bride**, who then symbolically hands her over to her new husband. Traditionally, the bride wears a **wedding dress** that is almost always in white. According to custom, brides must follow an old song that goes:

Something old and something new
Something borrowed and something blue.

As a result, some brides may feature a family heirloom as "the old," such as necklaces or earrings; the "borrowed" item is usually a handkerchief in case the bride weeps. The "blue" item is often the bride's garter. The "new", of course, would refer to the wedding gown itself, which can be quite extravagant with lace veils, crowns and/or long trains.

Before the person presiding over the wedding, the couple will usually **exchange vows** and then **wedding rings** made of gold. Once the ceremony is completed, the couple is **pronounced** "**man and wife**" and they begin the **recessional**, or departure of the married couple. As they walk back down the aisle together in their new status as newlyweds, the pianist or organist plays "**Wedding March**" by Felix Mendelssohn.

The Wedding Reception

After the wedding, the guests gather at a nearby location with invited family and friends come to eat and celebrate with the married couple. As the couple leaves the church or sanctuary, guests may **throw rice** at them as a symbol of fertility. The car that transports them to the reception is often decorated with cans tied to the bumper and a sign that reads, "**Just Married**!" At the reception, there is usually a band or DJ performing music and a wedding cake that is served after dinner. **Toasts** are made to the bride and groom with champagne by the best man and maid of honor, respectively. The couple will often jointly hold a knife to perform the **cutting of the wedding cake** together. They often feed a piece to each other. For fun, some couples have been known to smash the cake into each other's faces! After the meal, the couple also share their first dance together.

Before the end of the reception, the bride performs the tradition of **the tossing of the bouquet**. Here, the bride throws her bouquet of flowers over her shoulder without looking to an assembled group of unmarried women. Whoever catches the wedding bouquet is said to be the next to marry. Likewise, the groom will throw the bride's garter to a group of unmarried men or bachelors.

Housing

In Theme II, Matthew, an English teacher (and Jennifer's boyfriend from Book I), is exhausted after countless nights of being kept up by his noisy neighbors. As his friend, Soyeong advises him to seek new housing, but Matthew confesses that he is at a loss as to how to go about it. Soyeong gives Matthew some suggestions and he decides to search the classified ads of English newspaper websites. After contacting another foreigner over the telephone, Matthew inquires about the apartment and learns that there is an opportunity to take over the foreigner's apartment. However, Matthew must try to negotiate the amount of the rent with both the landlord and his *hagweon* owner.

Moving

Soyeong Hey, Matt. You look beat.

Matthew I hardly slept a wink last night.

Soyeong Rough night?

Matthew It's my upstairs neighbors. They kept me up all night. I've tried talking nicely to them and even complained to my landlord, but it's no use. They make such a racket!

Soyeong **You do know** that you can always move into a new apartment, **don't you?** I know it's a hassle, but why torture yourself if you're this unhappy?

Matthew Yeah, I've been thinking about that. But the problem is, I don't know how to go about it. **Do you know where the best** place is to look for an apartment in Seoul?

Soyeong Most people either use a *budongsan junggyesa* or check online using the Internet. **I've heard that** a *budongsan* agent is your best bet, especially for a foreigner like you.

Matthew Wait a minute. What's a *budongsan junggyesa*?

Soyeong   That's Korean for "real estate agent." They have offices in almost every neighborhood and work on commission. All you have to do is tell them what you're looking for in terms of price, space and whatnot.

Matthew   That would be great. **All I need is** a quiet room with easy access to the subway and I should be fine.

Soyeong   You could also check out the classified ads in the English-language newspapers and websites for foreigners in Seoul. I know that expats sometimes post their apartments for sale.

Matthew   Thanks, Soyeong. I think I'll shoot for the classified ads.

Key Patterns

1. I've heard that~
   I've heard that a *budongsan* agent is your best bet.

2. You do know~, don't you?
   You do know that you can always move into a new apartment, don't you?

3. All I need is~
   All I need is a quite room with easy access to the subway.

4. Do you know where the best place is to~?
   Do you know where the best place is to look for an apartment in Seoul?

1

I've heard that _____.   저는 _____라고 들었어요.

I've heard that a *budongsan* agent is your best bet.

I've heard that~ 은 직접적으로 혹은 간접적으로 들어서 알고 있는 사실에 대해서 이야기하는 구문입니다.

A. I've heard that + 주어 + 동사: 저는 ~라고 들었어요.

I've heard that a *budongsan* (real estate) agent is your best bet, especially for a foreigner like you.

당신과 같은 외국인이라면 특히나, 부동산 중개인이 제일 적합하다고 들었어요.

You do know _____, don't you?　　　_____ 그럴죠?

You do know that you can always move into a new apartment, don't you?

You do know~, don't you?는 부가의문문이라고 할 수 있습니다. 부가의문문은 크게 2가지 뜻을 가집니다. 첫 번째로는 '그럴죠?'라는 의문의 뜻, 두 번째로는 '그렇잖아요'라는 동의를 받고자 하는 경우입니다. 각각 올라가는 억양과 내려가는 억양으로 내용을 파악할 수 있습니다. 형태상으로 만드는 방법을 살펴보면, 앞 동사의 종류와 시제를 잘 파악해서, 일반 동사라면 do를, be 동사와 have 동사라면 각각 잘 맞춰서 사용해야 합니다. 물론 긍정과 부정이 바뀐다는 것도 이해하셔야겠지요.

You do know that you can always move into a new apartment, don't you? 당신은 언제든지 새로운 아파트로 이사를 갈 수 있다고요, 알죠?

All I need is _____.　　 내게 진짜 필요한 것은 _____.

All I need is a quiet room with easy access to the subway.

All I need is~ 문형은 이전에 다루었던 The important thing is~라는 구문과 비슷합니다. "내게 진짜 필요한 것은~"이라는 뜻으로 뒤에 곧장 명사가 와도 되고, 접속사 + 주어 + 동사가 오는 형식도 가능합니다.

A.　All I need is~: 내게 진짜 필요한 것은~

All I need is a quiet room with easy access to the subway.
제게 필요한 것은 지하철과 가까운 조용한 방뿐입니다.
All I need is your love.
제게 필요한 것은 당신의 사랑뿐이라고요.

B. All I need is + 접속사 + 주어 + 동사: 필요한 것은?

All I need is for him to understand me. 내게 필요한 것은 그가 나를 이해한다는 거예요.

4

Do you know where the best place is to~?

어디서 ＿＿＿＿＿＿＿ 한지 아세요?

Do you know where the best place is to look for an apartment in Seoul?

Do you know 다음에 who/when/where/what/why/how 등 육하원칙에 해당하는 의문사를 넣어서 다양한 간접의문문을 만들어 보겠습니다.

A. Do you know who~: 누가 ~한지 아세요?

Do you know who left this present? 누가 이 선물을 두고 갔는지 알아요?

B. Do you know when~: 언제 ~한지 아세요?

Do you know when she comes? 그녀가 언제쯤 올지 알 수 있을까?

C. Do you know where~: 어디서 ~한지 아세요?

Do you know where the best place is to look for an apartment in Seoul? 서울에서 아파트를 찾기 위한 가장 좋은 곳이 어딘지 아세요?

D. Do you know what~: 무엇을 ~한지 아세요?

Do you know what we're going to do? 우리가 무엇을 할지 상상이 가나요?

E. Do you know why~: 왜 ~한지 아세요?

Do you know why they left without saying goodbye?

그들은 왜 인사도 안 하고 그냥 간지 아세요?

F. Do you know how~: 어떻게 ~한지 아세요?

Do you know how to get the nearest subway station from here?

가장 가까운 지하철역으로 어떻게 갈 수 있는지 아세요?

Alternative Expressions

1

Rough night (insomnia)
= I didn't sleep well.
= I didn't get any sleep last night.
= I was up all night.
= I didn't sleep a wink.
= I pulled an all-nighter.
Also(opposite: to sleep):
= get some sleep
= get 40 winks
= get some shut-eye

2

hassle = a pain in the neck/butt
Be (a bit of) trouble.
Be a pain.

3

I don't know how to go about it.
= I don't know where to start.
= I don't know how to begin.
= I don't even know where to begin.

4

Wait a minute.
= Hold on.
= Just a sec(ond).
= Wait a minute.
= Whoa.

5

Commission

A commission is a fee or percentage for each sale that a salesperson or employee makes. We can use the phrase, "work(s) on commission."

6

All I want is~

= All I require is~

= All I ask is~

7

"easy access to the subway" means~

= A nearby subway

= Close to the subway

= Near the subway

= A subway that is close by

8

shoot for

= go for

= aim for

= take a stab at it = to try something

= head for(directional)

= eyeing for

= eye on the prize/eye on the ball

1. 잠을 못 잤다고? rough night? (insomnia)

불면증은 영어로도 한 단어입니다. insomnia이에요. 2008년에는 영국 가수 Craig David가, 2009년에는 휘성이라는 한국 가수가 아시아를 상대로 부른 노래제목이기도 하고요. "뭐야 뒤척이면서 잠을 못 잔 거라고?"라는 표현은 그럼 어떻게 하면 좋을까요?

● 잘 못 잤다고요? Rough night?
● 잘 못 잤어요. I didn't sleep well.
● 어젯밤 전혀 못 잤습니다. I didn't get any sleep last night.
● 밤새 내내 깨어 있었어요. I was up all night.
● 한숨도 못 잤어요. I didn't sleep a wink.
● 완전히 샜어요. I pulled an all-nighter.

2. 왜 그렇게 힘들게 하는데? Why torture yourself?

실제로 그만큼 심각한 것은 아닌데, 오히려 일을 어렵게 만드는 경우를 의외로 많이 봅니다. 스스로를 돕는 것이 아니라 스스로를 괴롭히는 거죠. 그럼 이럴 때 얘기하는 겁니다. "힘들게 하지 말고 그냥 좀 두면 안 될까?"라고요.

- Why make yourself miserable?
- Why make it (any) harder (than it has to be)?

Checking the Place Out

Tenant   Hello?

Matthew   Hi, I saw your advertisement in *The Korea Herald*. I'm interested in your apartment. Is it still available?

Tenant   Yes, it is. It's a small 66-square meter studio, but it has a washing machine and includes Internet access. I've only been here for a month, but I need someone to take over my lease. I promised the landlord I would do this for him.

Matthew   And how are the walls? Are they thick?

Tenant   Uh, I guess so. They're made of really solid material, if that's what you mean.

Matthew   Whew! That's a relief!

Tenant   **What makes you** say that?

Matthew   You would not believe my upstairs neighbors. The walls are paper-thin. I swear I can hear them coughing. I couldn't take it anymore! It would be OK if they were quiet, but they like to party into the wee hours. It's been killing me!

Tenant	Oh, I see. Well, you don't have to worry about the neighbors here. They're as quiet as mice.
Matthew	Now the ad says the monthly rent is about 650,000 won per month and I would have to deposit 10 million won in key money. What about utilities?
Tenant	You'd have to pay your own utilities such as electricity, water and gas. There's also a maintenance fee of 50,000 won per month. That's for your security guard and general maintenance.
Matthew	**That's a little on the steep side.** My *hagweon* will take care of the key money, but I don't know if I have that kind of money for monthly rent.
Tenant	Why don't you ask the owner if he's willing to reduce the rent a little if your *hagweon* pays a little more for the key money?
Matthew	**I wish I could** do that. But I don't know. Do you think they would be willing to do that?
Tenant	**You might as well** try. It's certainly worth asking. The landlord has a lot of foreign tenants. He knows what it's like for us. I don't know about your *hagweon*, though.
Matthew	Hmm, I guess I've got nothing to lose by asking. If we could negotiate something where I could reduce my rent by even 100,000 won, I'd be able to manage that.

Key Patterns

1. I wish I could~   I wish I could do that.

2. You might as well~   You might as well try.

3. That's a little on the~ side~
   That's a little on the steep side.

4. What makes you~?   What makes you say that?

1

I wish I could _____. _____이면 정말 좋을 텐데.

I wish I could do that.

I wish I could~는 가정법 구문으로, "~이면 정말 좋을 텐데"라는 뜻을 담고 있습니다.
I wish I could~뿐만 아니라, wish to~, wish (that), wish + someone + something
까지 확대시켜 배워봅시다. 마지막 표현은 노래로도 많이 들어보셨을 겁니다.

A. I wish I could + 동사 원형: ~이면 좋겠습니다.

A: Why don't you ask the owner if he's willing to reduce the
   rent a little?
   주인에게 혹시 월 임대료를 좀 내려주실 의향이 있는지 물어보면 어떨까요?

B: I wish I could do that. But I don't know.
   그렇게 할 수 있다면 좋겠습니다. 그런데 잘 모르겠어요.

I wish I could help you, Jason.
제이슨 씨, 저도 당신을 돕고 싶습니다.

I wish I could play the piano like that.
나도 그렇게 피아노 치고 싶어.

B. I wish to + 동사 원형: ~이면 좋겠습니다.

I wish to stay with you over the weekend.
주말을 너랑 함께 있으면 좋겠어.

C. I wish (that) + 주어 + 동사: ~가 ~하면 좋겠습니다.

I wish (that) it were that easy.
나는 그것이 그처럼 쉬웠으면 하고 바라고 있어.
I wish she had told me you were visiting.
네가 방문하는 것을 그녀가 미리 말해주었으면 좋았을 텐데.

D. I wish + someone + something: ~에게 ~를 기원합니다.

I wish you a Merry Christmas. 즐거운 성탄~
I wish you a happy birthday. 생일 축하드립니다.

2

You might as well _____. _____ 할지도 몰라.
You might as well try.

You might as well + 동사 원형~ 구문은 조동사 might의 뜻을 정확히 이해하는 것부터 시작합니다. might를 단순히 may의 과거형으로만 이해하는 학생들이 많은데, 실제로는 현재시제로도 자주 사용되며, 앞, 뒤 문맥을 통해 정확한 시제를 알 수 있는 경우도 많습니다.

우선 might가 조동사로서, "추측이나 허가, 가능성"의 뜻이 있다는 점을 기억하시고, may보다는 다소 확률이 떨어진다는 것도 익혀둡니다. 조동사는 표현에 특별히 "맛"을 더합니다. 기초를 넘어 『영어회화 II』를 배우는 여러분은 당연히 꼭 배워두셔야 합니다.

A. You might as well + 동사 원형: ~할지도 몰라.

You might as well try. It's certainly worth asking. The landlord has a lot of foreign tenants.

한 번 시도해보는 것이 좋을 듯한데. 물어볼 가치는 분명히 있어. 주인은 외국인 입주자들이 많거든.

B. 주어 + might + 동사 원형: 아마도 ~할지도 몰라, ~일 거야.

He might not get in touch with me.

그는 내게 연락을 안 할지도 몰라.

Your laptop might be in the office.

당신의 노트북은 아마도 사무실에 있을 거예요.

3

That's a little on the _____ side _____.

_____한 경향이 있다.

That's a little on the steep side.

평서문 구문은 ~a little on the~ side로, '~한 경향이 있다'는 표현입니다.

A: **There's also a maintenance fee of 50,000 won per month.**
그 외에도 한 달에 5만 원씩 관리비가 있어요.

B: **That's a little on the steep side.**
좀 비싼 경향이 있는데요.

What makes you _____?

당신은 왜 _____ 하나요?

What makes you say that?

What makes you~?는 "당신은 왜 ~하나요?", "무엇이 당신으로 하여금 ~하게 했습니까?"라는 구문입니다. 쉽게 '왜, 어떤 이유로 당신은 ~하세요?' 라고 원인과 결과에 대한 질문이 되겠죠. 현재형 동사가 오는 경우, 형용사, 그리고 과거형까지 3 가지 문형으로 익혀보겠습니다.

A. What makes you + 동사 원형: 당신은 왜 ~하세요?

What makes you say that?

왜 그렇게 말씀하세요?

What makes you continue that job?

무엇 때문에 그 일을 계속하고 계십니까?

B. What makes you + 형용사: 당신 왜 ~그러세요?

What makes you happy?

당신은 어떤 일로 행복해하십니까?

What makes you sure that's him?

도대체 왜 그라고 확신하시는 거예요?

C. What made you + 동사 원형: 어떤 계기로, 혹은 이유로 ~하게 되었나요?

What made you become interested in English?

어떤 계기로 영어에 흥미를 가지시게 됐어요?

What made you change your mind?

너 왜 맘을 바꿨어?

Alternative Expressions

1

Is it still available?

= Is it still on/up for/for sale?　　= Is it still on the market?

2

I couldn't take it anymore!

= I couldn't bear it (any longer).

= I couldn't endure it.

= It drove me crazy.

= It drove me nuts.

3

a little

= a (tiny) bit　　　　　= a tad

= a smidgen

4

He knows what it's like for us.

= He understands our circumstance.

= He's understanding.

= He's sympathetic to our plight.

= He has experience dealing with our situation.

= He can relate to us.

5

manage that

= afford that　　　　　= swing that

= we could do that　　　= that would work

1. 진짜 늦은 시간 wee hours

우리가 시간에 대해서 알고 있는 표현은 사실 아침, 점심, 저녁, 그리고 새벽 정도입니다. 한밤이라고 해도 그냥 late at night 정도로 사용하죠. 이번에 좀더 생생하게 "한밤중에 파티나 하고 시끄러워 죽겠다"는 좀더 격한 감정을 배워볼까요?

● I hate my upstairs neighbors. They always party into the wee hours. They were so noisy last night, so I had to call the police.
나 위층 사는 사람들 너무 싫어. 진짜 늦은 시간에 늘 파티를 한다니까. 어젯밤에 너무 시끄러워서 결국 경찰에 신고했어.
● 밤늦은 시간에 In the dead of night
● 한밤중에 In the middle of the night

2. 계속해봐! 움직이라고! Moving on!

move on을 두 가지로 알아보겠습니다. 첫 번째는 이야기를 계속하라는 뜻입니다. 그래서 '다음은?' 이라고 할 때 moving on!뿐만 아니라 continuing on, 혹은 moving along, 쉽게 next를 사용하면 적절합니다. 혹시 교통 경찰관이 "Move on!"이라고 했다면 무슨 뜻일까요? 그렇죠. 자동차라면 서 있지 말고, 가라는 뜻이 되겠습니다.
move on의 두 번째 뜻은 다음 단계로 나아가라는 뜻이 되는데, 남녀 관계에서 이혼, 사별, 혹은 친구랑 헤어졌거나, 회사일로나 여러 가지 힘든 일을 겪고 있을 때 어느 정도 시간이 흐른 후 극복하고 나아가라고 하는 것이 좋은 예가 되겠습니다.

● Please forget about James. It's time to move on. It's better for you, Shannon. 제임스를 잊고 용서해. 이제 잊을 때도 됐잖아. 다 너를 위한 거야, 섀년.
● Let's move on to the next level! 다음 단계로 나아가자고!

Exercises

• Collocation Match-Up

Collocations are special combinations of words that can be idioms or other phrases and expressions. Find collocations from Lessons 3 and 4 by matching the words from Column A which best match with the words in Column B.

A.	B.
1. best ·	· to
2. wee ·	· bet
3. be willing ·	· for
4. shoot ·	· lose
5. slept ·	· night
6. nothing to ·	· hours
7. rough ·	· a wink

The American poet Walt Whitman once said, "A man is not a whole and complete man unless he owns a house and the ground it stands." Indeed, the idea of home ownership is deeply ingrained in the minds of Americans today as a symbol of comfort, security, family and the achievement of the American Dream. In the classic

movie "The Wizard of Oz," Dorothy says, "There's no place like home!" Most Americans know the popular song "Home on the Range" (which is also the official state song of Kansas) and everyone knows the expression, "Home Sweet Home!"

According to *The Wall Street Journal*, more than two-thirds of all Americans own their own homes. Among Caucasians, more than 75 percent are **homeowners**. However, this was not always the case in American history.

Before the 20th century, home **mortgages** were not common. In fact, less than half of all Americans owned homes and from 1900 to 1930, the rate of home ownership actually decreased. In the past, lenders would give only extremely high interest rates to people who wanted to purchase a house. Also, the terms for the interest rates were very short—only three to five years. Thus, most Americans either built their own homes or simply rented houses. In short, it was cheaper to rent than to buy!

The Great Depression during the 1930s, however, completely changed the way the U.S. government intervened in the economy. In response to the crisis, the government passed laws and policies that enabled it to radically intervene in the housing market. The Federal Housing Administration was created in 1934, reducing interest rates and setting mortgage terms for 25 and 30 years. The result was that it was easier and more possible for American citizens to purchase their own homes. After World War II, there was a huge population explosion known as the "**Baby Boom**," and more families began settling in the **suburbs**—outlying regions from the city characterized by single-family houses that were less crowded and more residential than the busy, central life of cities.

In addition, a massive network of highways and roads began to be constructed. That coupled with the meteoric rise of the automobile made Americans more mobile than ever. As a result, people began to move further and further away from city centers, and a need and demand rose for more housing. By the 1950s, with the help of government-supported loan programs and policies, more than half of all Americans owned homes for the first time in history. By the 1960s, it became cheaper to own a house than to rent.

Of course, home ownership did not proceed smoothly. Blacks and other minorities often faced more difficulty in securing mortgages and tended to be left behind in the inner cities while the mostly White population moved to the suburbs. Still, the housing phenomenon was powerful, giving images of a front yard, a sidewalk, a tree-lined street and most of all, **a white picket fence**. These became the symbols of comfort and security for a middle-class suburb.

Here are some expressions that convey the powerful notion of "home" in America:

Home Sweet Home!

I feel at home with~: to be comfortable or relaxed with

Be at home with~: to be comfortable or relaxed with

be close to home~: to be quite familiar or intimate with oneself

Make yourself at home~: An expression used to make a guest or visitor feel comfortable and at ease

There's no place like home~: Home is the best place for comfort and rest.

Home free~: to successfully free oneself of a burden, duty or problem; to feel relief and freedom

A man's home is his castle~: A man feels like a king in his own home.

Getting Around Seoul

Lesson 5

Lost in Itaewon

Lesson 6

ATM

Lesson 7

International Clinic

Theme III takes us on the encounters of three foreigners in Seoul: Mary, Steven and Evan. First, Mary and Steven have just arrived as tourists to Seoul, but have become lost in Itaewon. In need of cash, they inquire about the nearest bank. Fortunately for them, Itaewon has enough foreigners who know their way around the neighborhood. One such foreigner is able to direct the couple to the closest bank. However, once there, Mary and Steven have trouble accessing the Automated Teller Machine (ATM) given that the directions are written in Korean. With the help of a friendly bank teller, they are finally able to withdraw cash. Switching the scene, another English teacher named Evan has been quite sick for several weeks. While initially hoping to avoid seeking medical treatment, he ends up going to an international clinic. There, a Dr. Kim informs Evan that he has a severe case of tonsillitis and needs rest.

Lost in Itaewon

Mary   It's getting to be around lunchtime. The first thing we need to do is get some cash. But nothing looks familiar on this map.

Steven   **I wonder where** we might find an ATM? Any ideas?

Mary   Well, we'll just be going around in circles if we continue like this. Let's try to ask someone. **It would save us** a lot of time. Oh, look! There's another foreigner. Let's ask her!

Steven   Excuse me, we're visiting Seoul and have kind of lost our bearings. **Would you happen to** know where we can find an ATM?

Foreigner   Sure. Try any bank. They usually have an ATM in their lobby. The closest one is around that corner. It's just a short walk.

Steven   **Which way is it**?

Foreigner   First, walk across the street. Take a left and you will eventually run into a bank. It has a blue and white sign.

Mary   Do you mind pointing out the way for us?

Foreigner   Not at all. See this street here? Just cross over to the other side. Then hang a left at the corner and keep walking straight for about 75 meters. You can't miss it.

Mary   Thanks a million! We really appreciate it!

Key Patterns

1. **I wonder~**
   I wonder where we might find an ATM.

2. **Would you happen to know~**
   Would you happen to know where we can find an ATM?

3. **It would save (us) a lot of~**   It would save us a lot of time.

4. **Which way (is it)?**   Which way is it?

1

I wonder _____ .   _____가 궁금해요.

I wonder where we might find an ATM.

I wonder~? 뒤에는 가장 흔히 if, whether + 주어 + 동사 구문이 나옵니다. 그 외에도 I wonder 다음에 where, when, why, what 등 다양한 의문사가 올 수 있습니다. 말 그대로 궁금하다는 표현인데, 질문은 그대로 하면서 간접의문문 형태가 되기 때문에, 자연스럽고 공손한 표현이 됩니다. 이메일에서도 직접적인 질문 대신에 자주 사용할 수 있는 구문이니, 꼭 잘 외워놓으세요.

A. I wonder + 의문사 (where, when, why, what): ~가 궁금해요.

I wonder where we might find an ATM.
우리가 어디서 현금자동인출기를 찾을 수 있을까요?
I wonder when they will get married.   그들이 언제 결혼할지 궁금해.
I wonder why coffee is popular.   커피가 왜 인기가 있는지 궁금합니다.
I wonder what movie to see.   무슨 영화를 볼까.
I wonder what went wrong.   무엇이 잘못되었는지 알고 싶어.

B. I wonder if/whether + 주어 + 동사: ~할지 궁금해요.

I wonder if you really love me. 당신이 나를 진심으로 사랑하는지 알고 싶소.
I wonder whether I can get a refund. 제가 환불을 받을 수 있는지 궁금합니다.

2

Would you happen to know _____?

당신은 혹시 _____룰 아세요?

Would you happen to know where we can find an ATM?

Would you happen to know + 의문사 + 주어 + 동사~? 구문입니다. Would라
는 조동사를 통해 공손함을 나타내고, 상대편이 아는지 모르는지 불확실한 상황이기
때문에 happen to라는 동사를 사용하였습니다. 위에서 언급한 I wonder 표현과 마
찬가지로 직접적인 질문을 우회적으로 하고 있는 구문입니다.

A. Would you happen to know 의문사 + 주어 + 동사~?: 당신은 혹시 ~를 아세요?

Would you happen to know where we can find an ATM?
혹시 당신은 우리가 어디서 현금자동인출기를 찾을 수 있을지 아십니까?
Would you happen to know when the movie starts?
혹시 영화 몇 시에 시작하는지 아세요?

3

It would save (us) a lot of _____.

많은 _____를 줄일 수 있을 겁니다.

It would save us a lot of time.

It would save (사람) a lot of + 명사 구문입니다. 이 표현 역시 would라는 조동사
가 공손하면서도 가정법의 느낌을 갖습니다. 그러므로 과거형 문장이 아니라 "~할
것이다"라고 해석하실 수 있어야 합니다.

A. It would save a lot of + 명사: 많은 ~를 줄일 수 있을 겁니다.

It would save us a lot of time and money.
우리는 시간과 돈을 절약할 수 있을 겁니다.
It would save him a lot of trouble. 그는 곤경에서 벗어날 수 있을 거예요.

4

Which way (is it)? 어느 방향으로요?
Which way is it?

Which way (is it)? 하면 당연히 어느 방향인지 갈 길을 묻는 표현이 되겠죠. it 자리에 다양한 명사를 넣는 것이 가장 쉬운 구문 연습입니다. 그리고 동사와 형용사로 내용을 확대시켜 배워보세요.

A. Which way + 동사 + 명사~?: 어느 길 (방향)로 ~하나요?

Which way is it? Do you mind pointing out the way for us?
어느 길로 갑니까? 혹시 저희에게 그 방향을 알려주시겠어요?
Which way is the bathroom/exit/market?
화장실/출구/시장은 어떤 길로 가나요?

B. Which way + 동사 + 형용사~ / 명사~?: 어떤 방법이 더 ~합니까?

Which way is better for me?
저에게 어느 방법이 더 좋겠습니까?
Which way do you recommend for me to take?
당신은 저에게 어느 방향을 택하라고 추천하시고 싶으신가요?

Alternative Expressions

1

Would you happen to know where we can find～?

= Do you know where we can locate～?

= Where might we find a～?

= Do you know where the closest～ is?

2

Going around in circles

= going nowhere fast

= going nowhere

= wasting our time

= spinning our wheels

3

lose one's bearings = to become confused

lose one's footing

lose one's grip

lose one's sense of direction

to be out of sorts

Opposite:

to get/gain one's bearings

Hang a left

go right/left

turn~

take a~

head~

make a right turn/left turn

take a little jog to the left/right

go straight

head straight

walk straight ahead

circle around

curve left/right

5

You can't miss it.

= It's standing right in front of you.

= It's right before you.

= It's right under your nose.

= It's obvious.

= It's as plain as day.

= It's easy to see.

= It's easy to find.

1. 그렇게 되지 않았어. 불행이야. No dice.

비록 간절히 바라긴 했지만 바라던 대로 이
루어지지 않은 일에 대해서 약간의 후회와
미련을 버리지 못하고 "불행이야"라고 말하
는데 영어로는 "No dice", 이렇게 표현합니
다. 한마디로 주사위는 굴러갔는데, 자신이
원하던 번호는 아니였던 거죠.

- It didn't work out.
- No luck.

2. 엎친 데 덮친 격이야. Rub salt in wounds.

불난 데 부채질하기 혹은 엎친 데 덮쳤다는 것은 어떻게 표현하면 좋을까요? 결국 상상
했던 것보다 상황이 더욱 악화되고 있다는 뜻인데요. '악화일로'를 영어로 아주 재미있
게 표현해봅니다. '상처 난 곳에 소금 바르기'예요. 혹시 양치를 소금으로 해보신 적 있
으세요? 물을 섞어도 멀쩡한 입안이 따끔거리는데 더군다나 상처 난 곳에 소금을 문지
른다고 상상을 해보세요. 그 상처가 아물기는커녕, 더 덧나지 않을까요?

- To make matters worse
- This will only make it worse.
- This only worsens it.

Lesson 6

ATM

Steven	Excuse me. **I was in the middle of** my transaction when this sign popped up in Korean. I can't seem to withdraw cash and I don't read Korean. **Where can I** get some help?
Bank Teller	Let's go to the lobby where I can assist you. Do you have your credit card with you?
Steven	Yes. It's right here. It's a foreign credit card so that might explain the problem.
Bank Teller	Ah, yes. That's often the case. **Do you mind if** I insert your card for you?
Steven	Please. Go right ahead.
Bank Teller	First, you have to press this button. This indicates that you are using a foreign card. This button gives you the option of having the directions listed in English.
Mary	I guess that's where we went wrong. **Let's try to** withdraw some cash now.
Bank Teller	Please enter your security code. [*Looks away as Steven enters his pass code.*]

Bank Teller   Finished? From here, it's simple. Just select the amount you wish to withdraw and press "*hwagin*." This means "confirm." To cancel, press "*chwiso*."

Mary   That was simple enough! Thank you so much! It was taking forever to get some cash!

Key Patterns

1. I was in the middle of~
   I was in the middle of my transaction when this sign popped up in Korean.

2. Do you mind if~
   Do you mind if I insert your card for you?

3. Let's try to~
   Let's try to withdraw some cash now.

4. Where can I ~?
   Where can I get some help?

1

I was in the middle of _____.

_____을 하고 있는 중이었다.

I was in the middle of my transaction when this sign popped up in Korean.

I was in the middle of + 동사의 명사형 혹은 명사가 오는 구문입니다. '~을 하고 있는 중이었다, 바빴다' 정도의 해석이 됩니다. 전화를 받지 못한 상황 등 나중에 자신이 그 당시에 대해 설명해야 하는 경우 유용합니다. 그리고 지금 당장 바쁠 때도 현재형으로 자유롭게 사용하세요.

A. I was in the middle of + 명사/동사의 명사형: ~하는 중이었습니다.

Excuse me. I was in the middle of my transaction when this sign popped up in Korean.
죄송합니다. 제가 기기 작동 중이었는데, 갑자기 한국어로 이런 표시나 나왔네요.
I was in the middle of reviewing documents for the presentation.
발표용 자료를 검토 중에 있었습니다.

B. I am in the middle of + 명사/동사의 명사형: ~하는 중입니다.

Sorry, I can't take your call right now. I am in the middle of a meeting. Can I call you back?

실례지만 지금 제가 전화를 받을 수 없습니다. 회의 중이에요. 나중에 전화를 드려도 될까요?

2

Do you mind if _____? (제가) _____ 해도 괜찮을까요?

Do you mind if I insert your card for you?

Do you mind if (I)~는 "(제가) ~해도 괜찮을까요"라고 묻는 구문입니다. 첫째, mind 동사의 뜻이 '~을 꺼리다'로 부정적입니다. 그러므로 이 구문은 대답하는 방식까지 올바로 이해하고 있어야 자유롭게 사용할 수 있습니다. 둘째, do you mind if + 주어 + 동사 형식과, do you mind + 동사~ing 형식 두 가지로 사용할 수 있도록 익힙니다. Do you mind 동사~ing는 상대방에게 허락을 구하거나 청할 때 사용합니다. 그리고 마지막으로 do you mind 구문 역시 상대편을 배려하는 형식의 의문문으로 활용도가 매우 높으니 꼭 기억하시기 바랍니다.

A. Do you mind if + 주어 + 동사: ~가 ~를 해도 괜찮을까요?, 될까요?

A: **Do you mind if I insert your card for you?**

제가 당신을 대신해서 당신 카드를 넣어봐도 괜찮으시겠습니까?

B: **Please. Go right ahead.**

그럼요. 그렇게 하세요.

A: **Do you mind if I sit there?**

제가 거기 좀 앉아도 되겠습니까?

B: **Of course not.**

물론이죠. 앉으세요.

Do you mind if we have company?

우리가 동행인을 데리고 가도 괜찮으시겠어요?

Do you mind if this is the last one?

이게 마지막인데 괜찮겠어?

B. Do you mind + 동사~ing: ~를 해도 괜찮을까요?

Do you mind washing the dishes?

당신 설거지 좀 해줄래요?

Do you mind staying?

당신 머무르시겠어요?

Do you mind my staying?

내가 머물러도 될까?

Let's try to _____. _____ 해봅시다.

Let's try to withdraw some cash now.

Let's try to~는 뭔가 함께 해보자는 제안의 구문입니다. 물론 Let's~ + 동사 역시 함께 하자는 뜻이 되지요. 그러나 try to가 동사 앞에 들어가면, 함께 뭔가를 해보자고, 안 되더라도 한 번은 시도해보자는 적극적인 느낌이 강해집니다. Let's dance! 하고 Let's try to dance! Let's figure out what it is! 하면 뜻이 좀 다른 것을 이해하실 수 있어요?

A. Let's try to + 동사 원형: (노력)해봅시다.

Let's try to withdraw some cash now.

그럼 현금을 인출해보도록 하죠.

Let's try to stay on a diet.

계속 다이어트를 합시다.

Let's try to forgive and forget.

(힘들겠지만 그래도) 용서하고 잊도록 노력해봅시다.

4

Where can I _____?

제가 _____ 를 하고 싶은데 어디로 가야 하나요?

Where can I get some help?

Where can I~ 동사 구문은 어디서 그 일을 할 수 있는지 장소를 물어보기 위해서 사용합니다. "제가 ~를 하고 싶은데 어디로 가야 하나요"라는 뜻이지요. 예문으로 익혀봅시다.

A. Where can I + 동사 원형: ~ 할 수 있는 곳이 어디입니까?

Where can I get some help?

제가 어디서 도움을 받을 수 있을까요?

Where can I buy a vacuum cleaner?

진공청소기는 어디서 살 수 있나요?

Where can I sleep?

저 어디서 자요?

Alternative Expressions

1

Other banking/ATM words:
inquiry
deposit
balance
(make a) wire transfer
password

2

that might explain
that might have something to with it
that might be the source [of your trouble]
that might be the culprit
that might be the trouble
that could be the cause
that could be why
that could be the reason why

3

gives [one] the option
= allows one the choice/option
= gives one the opportunity
      the choice of
= provides [you] the option
         chance
         opportunity

4

it's simple.

= it's a snap.

= it's a piece of cake.

= it's easy as pie.

= it's as easy as ABC.

5

take forever

= It's so slow.

= It's dragging on (and on).

= It's going at a snail's pace.

= It's going at a crawl. ~[traffic]

1. 진짜 웃겨! LOL

여러분이 가장 흔하게 사용하는 문자 약어는
뭐가 있을까요? 한때 움짤, 짤방은 말할 것도
없고, ㅋㅋ 혹은 ㅎㅎ, 이멜, 수욜 등 다양한
표현을 사용하셨을 겁니다. 이 시간에는 "진
짜 웃긴다"에 해당하는 3가지 표현과, 몇 가
지 유용하면서도 간단한 영어 약어 표현을 살
펴보겠습니다.

- LOL: Laugh Out Loud
- LMAO: Laughing My Ass Off
- ROFL: Rolling On the Floor Laughing
- ASAP: As Soon As Possible
- BTW: By the Way
- CU@Coffee bin TMRW: See You at Coffee Bean tomorrow

2. 진짜 비싸요. An arm and a leg

"진짜 비싸요" 역시 가장 쉽게는 "It's very expensive"라고 표현하시면 됩니다. 그런
데 영어로 매우 흥미로운 표현이 있거든요. "팔과 다리에요"라는 영어표현은 "백만 불짜
리 각선미 보험을 들으셨군요"라고 생각하세요. 그러면 "It's an arm and a leg"을 "비
싸군요"로 잘 해석하실 수 있을 겁니다.

- It cost us a pretty penny.
- It wasn't cheap!
- This is going to leave a lot of damage in its wake.

International Clinic

Dr. Kim   Hi Evan, I'm Dr. Kim. Please have a seat on the examining table. **I understand that** you're not feeling well. What are your symptoms?

Evan   Hi, Doc. I have a high fever and a sore throat. I'm also really exhausted. The fatigue seems to come out of nowhere. In the middle of the day, I'll suddenly feel exhausted. I've been knocked out for the past few days with pain relievers and can barely get out of bed.

Dr. Kim   That doesn't sound good. **Since when did** you first start feeling like this?

Evan   Well, it's been on and off for a few weeks now, but I think it first started back about a month ago.

Dr. Kim   Let me check your throat first. Could you open your mouth and say "Ah"?

Evan   Ahhhh～

Dr. Kim   It looks like you've got tonsillitis. A pretty nasty case, too. It's quite swollen and your tonsils are enlarged.

Evan   That's nothing! You should have seen my throat a few days ago. It was so swollen that I could barely swallow!

Dr. Kim   Next time, I'd advise you to seek help sooner with a condition like this. If you put off seeing a doctor, the consequences can sometimes be serious.

Evan   Really? I suppose you're right. I figured I'd try to stick it out for as long as I could and just put up with the pain, but I can see that it could do more harm than good in the long run.

Dr. Kim   That's exactly right. I'll prescribe some antibiotics. It should clear up in a week or so.

Evan   Hey Doc. I was planning on going on vacation with my wife next week. Do you think it would still be OK to travel?

Dr. Kim   **You're better off** staying at home and resting. This illness is probably stress-related. Get some rest and drink lots of fluids.

Evan   What a drag! I was just really hoping to make it to Thailand.

Dr. Kim   **I'd be more worried about** getting back on my feet than lying out on the beach if I were you!

Key Patterns

1. **I understand that~**
   I understand that you're not feeling well.

2. **You're better off~**
   You're better off staying at home and resting.

3. **I'd be (more) worried about~ (than)**
   I'd be more worried about getting back on my feet than laying out on the beach!

4. **Since when did you~?**
   Since when did you first start feeling like this?

1

I understand that _____ . _____ 하시다는 거군요.

I understand that you're not feeling well.

I understand that + 주어 + 동사~ 구문은 상대편이 말한 내용에 대해서 '동의한다, 이해한다', 그러면서 이야기를 이어가는 표현입니다. 대화란 결국 2인 이상의 사람이 각자의 이야기를 하는 것이고, 상대편의 반응에 따라 풍성해지기도 하고, 금방 끝나기도 합니다. 여러분은 어떤 대화를 원하십니까?

A. I understand that + 주어 + 동사: ~ 하시다는 거군요.

   A: **I understand that you're not feeling well. What are your symptoms?** 당신이 상태가 좋지 않다는 점 이해가 갑니다. 증상이 어때요?

B: I have a high fever and a sore throat.

열이 높고, 목이 아파요.

I understand that you wouldn't hurt her.

당신이 그녀를 아프게 하고 싶지 않다는 것 이해해요.

B. It's my understanding that~/It has come to my attention that~: 제가 이해하기로는~

It's my understanding that you're pursuing your Ph.D. program in Journalism. 저는 당신이 언론학 박사 과정 중에 있는 것으로 알고 있어요.

It has come to my attention that he has talked with the boss about the raise. 그가 사장과 임금 협상에 관해 이미 이야기를 나누었다는 점이 눈길을 끌었어요.

2

You are better off _____. _____ 하면 더 나아지다.
You're better off staying at home and resting.

You are better off~는 우선 be better off~를 이해하셔야 하는데, '전보다 살림살이가 나아지다, 형편이 나아지다, 혹은 전보다 잘 지내다'라는 뜻을 갖고 있습니다. 그 다음으로 off를 부사로 사용하면서 동사를 be 대신 had를 바꿔봅니다. 제안을 하고 싶다면, you had better 동사/if + 주어 + 동사 표현도 유용합니다. 친구나 동료 사이에 가볍게 충고를 해야 할 경우도 사용할 수 있지만 보다 정확하게는 상대방에게 어떤 일을 하라고 강하게 권하는 명령이나 권고라고 할 수 있으니, 상대방이 상사나 윗사람인 경우보다는 나보다 나이가 어리거나 편한 친구관계 정도일 때 사용하세요.

A. You are better off + 명사: ~ 하면 더 나아지다.

A: Do you think it would still be OK to travel?

여행을 하는 것이 괜찮을까요?

B: You're better off staying at home and resting.

집에서 쉬는 것이 더 나을 것 같습니다.

You're better off calling her to say sorry.

전화해서 그녀에게 미안하다고 말하는 편이 더 좋겠습니다.

You would be the better for it. 당신은 그렇게 하시는 편이 더 좋을 것 같아요.

It would probably be better if you make a new plan.

새로운 계획을 세우신다면 더 좋을 것 같습니다.

B. You had better + 동사: ~ 하도록 하시지요.

You'd better have a good attitude. 올바른 태도로 좀 얌전하게 있어라.

You'd better not get involved in this. 여기에는 끼어들지 않는 편이 좋겠어.

I think you'd better join the basketball team.

내 생각에는 네가 농구부에 들어가야 할 것 같구나.

3

I'd be (more) worried about _____ (than).

_____을 걱정하다.

I'd be more worried about getting back on my feet than laying out on the beach!

I'd be (more) worried about~ (than)은 세 가지 구문이 함께 있으니 각각을 이해해야 합니다. 우선 be worried about~은 '~을 걱정하다' 라는 표현입니다. 그리고 두 번째 more A than B는 B보다는 A라는 비교급 표현이 되겠죠. 그리고 마지막으로 would라는 조동사 덕분에 '~할 것이다' 라는 느낌을 갖게 됩니다.

A. be worried about~/be worried that~:~을 걱정하다.

I'm really worried about you. 저는 진심으로 당신을 걱정하고 있어요.

You're worried about the dress you lost?

넌 겨우 네가 잃어버린 옷 걱정이나 하고 있는 거야?

B. more A than B: B보다는 A

I drink more coffee than water. 물보다는 커피를 마실려고.
She loves Keane more than Oasis.
그녀는 오아시스보다는 킨을 더 좋아해. (Keane, Oasis 모두 영국 밴드명)

C. 조동사 would (be): ~할 것이다.

I'd be more worried about getting back on my feet than lying out on the beach!
제가 당신이 해변에서 누워 있는 것보다 다 나아오는 것을 걱정해야 하다니요.
I would be satisfied with your remodeling process.
당신의 재건축 과정에 대체적으로 만족할 것 같습니다.

4

Since when did you _____?

언제부터 _____ 되셨습니까?

Since when did you first start feeling like this?

Since when did you~?는 뭔가 불만이 있는 부정적인 표현으로 흔하게 사용됩니다. "그래서 도대체 언제부터 이렇게 되었는데?"라는 느낌이 오시나요?

A. Since when did you~?: 언제부터 ~되셨습니까?

Since when did you first start feeling like this?
도대체 언제부터 이런 증상을 느끼셨나요?
Since when have I ever lied to you?
언제부터 내가 당신에게 거짓말을 했다고 하시는 거예요?
Since when did you become such a liar?
당신은 도대체 언제부터 이렇게 거짓말쟁이가 된 거예요?

Alternative Expressions

1

out of nowhere
= from nowhere
= from out of thin air
= all of a sudden
= out of the blue

2

on and off
= comes and goes
= It's sporadic.
= It's intermittent.
= It's occasional.
= It's infrequent.
= on-again, off-again
= here and there

3

put off
= delay
= postpone

4

stick it out
= to endure
= bear with it
Also similar to "put up with"

5

It should clear up.

= It should get better.

= It should lighten up. [weather]

= It should improve.

= It should take care of itself.

6

What a drag!

= What a bummer!

= What a downer!

= That sucks!

Real & Live

1. 저는 모범생입니다. I'm a model student.

세 단계로 나누어서 설명해보겠습니다. 진짜 모범생
입니다. 누군가 역할 모델로서 본받을 만한 부분이
있다는 것이니, 다른 사람들에게 완벽해 보이겠죠?

- I'm a perfect student.
- Rebecca is a model student.

그런데 모범생 대신 '범생이'라고 할 때는 말하는 사람의 상대편에 대한 약간은 무시하
는 태도 그리고 비꼬는 면이 보이지요. 그러나 MS사의 Bill Gates가 nerd의 전형이라
고 한다면요? 어릴 때 좀 정신없이 자기 세계에만 몰두했으니 말입니다. nerd는 원래의
뜻인 부정적인 괴짜에서 약간 앞뒤가 막히긴 했지만 공부는 잘하는 범생이로 긍정적으
로 격상된 표현입니다.

- Hey, Jonathan, you're such a nerd.
- You know what, I love nerdy guys.

이번에는 손댈 수 없는 빤질이와 정말 심한 괴짜를 알아봅니다. 각각 geek와 dork라는
표현을 사용하는데 둘 다 다소 부정적인 표현이라는 점은 지나칠 수 없겠죠?

- I don't like to talk with Alan. He's such a geek.
- Eric is such a dork. How did he get a girlfriend?

2. 데이트에서 기초 중의 기초라고. Dating Manners 101

기초 중의 기초, 기본 중의 기본을 영어로 어떻게 표현하면 좋을까요? 벌써 basic이나 foundation 등 한국어를 그대로 영어로 옮긴 단어를 찾고 있지는 않나요? 기본 중의 기본을 101이라고 하는데 미국의 대부분 대학교에서 introduction 과목을 101으로 부르면서 생긴 표현입니다. 보통 1학년 과목은 1로 2, 3, 4학년 과목은 주로 백 단위가 2, 3, 4로 시작하거든요.

예를 들어보죠. 심리학 입문, 혹은 언어학 개론이라면 Introduction to Psychology 101, Introduction to Linguistics 101이 되겠죠. 누군가가 Economics 404를 듣는다면 4학년 이상의 전공과목일 확률이 높고, 이미 101 등의 선수 과목은 다 배웠다고 가정할 수 있겠습니다. 저 역시 대학원 과목에서 Qualitative Research 611, Topical Seminar 925 등을 들었던 기억이 납니다.

이 표현이 실제 과목명뿐만 아니라 일반적인 상황에서도 적절하게 사용되는 예를 살펴볼까요? '한국에서는 식사 때 젓가락을 사용합니다. 식당에서 신을 벗어야 하는 경우도 있을 겁니다', Life in Korea 101. '운전할 때, 특히 차선을 바꾸실 때는 앞뒤는 물론 양 옆을 꼭 확인하세요. 사각지대까지요', Driving 101. 첫 데이트에서 여성분을 차에 태우실 때는 혹시 멋쩍더라도 그녀를 위해서 차문을 열어주세요. 가능하다면 현관문이나 다른 문도요', Dating Manners 101입니다.

Exercises

Error correction

1. Which way it is?

2. It look like you' ve got tonsillitis.

3. Do you have your credit card for you?

4. You should have see my throat a few days ago.

5. Hang a left on the corner and keep walking straight.

6. We are visiting to Seoul and have kind of lost our bearings.

7. This button allows to you the option of having the directions listed in English.

South Korea is increasingly the country of choice for many English-speaking tourists and visitors. While most tourism to this country continues to come from such nearby Asian places as Japan, China, Taiwan, or Hong Kong, there have been many native English instructors from the West who consider Seoul, the Capital of South Korea, to be an ideal choice for working abroad. For example, many websites advertising jobs to prospective English teachers will

tout the convenient and modern aspects of areas such as Bundang, Gangnam and other places in and around Seoul that appeal to foreign sensibilities. In the Seocho area of Seoul, for example, the government has sponsored a project to make the area more amenable to its foreign residents. According to *The Korea Times*, the government is investing funds to construct wider sidewalks, narrower roads and more street lights. While there are always some who complain, foreign teachers for the most part seem to enjoy South Korea's living standards. They cite the convenient public transportation systems, the relatively cheap cost of living, the favorable pay scale and most of all, the prevalence of English-friendly signs and services that make it easier than other Asian countries for native English speakers to get around. In fact, a recent 2009 survey by Seoul City showed that many of these particular foreign expatriates responded more favorably to living in Seoul than native Koreans!

There have been a number of rapid and sophisticated upgrades that make South Korea more amenable to foreigners. **Incheon International Airport** has been voted the best airport in the world since 2005. Its facilities are very foreigner-friendly as signs are almost ubiquitously written in English and Korean. Also highly praised are the airport limousine buses that conveniently transport visitors to virtually any major part of Seoul for a nominal fee.

Once in Seoul, visitors note the extensive **Seoul subway system**. All directional signs and maps are printed in both English and Korean as well as in Chinese characters. People often remark on how easy it is to make one's way around the city. With a total of eleven lines and easily marked exits and transfer centers, it was one of the fastest and well-operated systems in the world. Seldom do visitors have to wait for more than five minutes for a train and usually for a fare that is less than $1. Compared to the fares in the U.S. which can run as much as $2.25 (New York City) to $3 (San Francisco), Seoul subway fares are some of the cheapest in the world at about 1,000 won per trip.

In addition to the subway, the **bus system** in South Korea has also been revamped to make transportation convenient. With the creation of bus-only lanes throughout the city and automated transportation cards that are compatible with the subway system, transportation in Seoul has never been easier. At many bus stops you can even find an electronic sign board that lists the bus number and the number of minutes till the next bus. And finally, while Seoul visitors will find that the city suffers from heavy traffic delays, the relative inexpensiveness of Korean **taxi cabs** compared with other parts of the world make it a viable option.

All in all, it's becoming easier to get around Seoul for foreigners. With "foreigner-friendly" tourist areas such as Itaewon, Insadong and Myeongdong, it's a good bet that the average native Korean is able to speak at least a smattering of English to guide and direct a foreigner given the country's mandatory English education curriculum in primary and secondary schools.

Most recently, South Korea has been touted as a country for **medical tourism**, and the number of foreigners seeking medical services has jumped in recent years. Medical tourism means to travel abroad to receive medical services which would otherwise be too expensive in one's native country. The United States, or example, suffers from a bloated, inefficient health care system that is highly unpopular, as can be seen in the 2007 documentary film "Sicko," by Michael Moore. The U.S. also has the most expensive health care costs in the world. With an estimated 50 million Americans without health insurance, President Barack Obama himself declared that "the skyrocketing cost of health care" was by far the greatest threat facing U.S. financial health. Thus, there has been an increasing number of Americans — especially Korean Americans and other ethnic Koreans abroad — who have sought out medical care in South Korea. Some of the larger hospitals such as Yonsei, Seoul National University and Samsung hospitals already feature international clinics. In addition to the advantages of world-class quality, care, and technology, the costs are said to be significantly cheaper here.

Cats and Dogs

In Theme IV, we explore the topic of household pets, and in particular, cats and dogs. Pets are extremely popular in North America and Europe. In this section, the discussion centers on cultural differences in attitudes toward certain animals as pets, particularly cats. As guests in Stella's home, Jason and Melissa are surprised to find that Stella would like to have cats, if only they were allowed. Jason and Melissa share a negative attitude toward cats and compare this with their experiences in Seoul.

At Stella's Apartment

Melissa	**This is such a** great pad you've got, Stella. I love how you decorated it. You're a real creature of comfort, eh?
Stella	You might say that. I had to scrounge around to find some of the furniture, but it all worked out in the end.
Jason	I've been checking out apartments myself. It's been quite a hassle trying to find a place that suits my needs. How did you manage to score such a nice place like this?
Stella	The university helped me out. The only thing I regret is that the landlord doesn't allow pets.
Melissa	I didn't know you were into pets! **Are you a** cat person **or a** dog person? I'm a dog person myself. I wish I had a dog here in Seoul.
Stella	Well, **I'd much rather** have a cat. I was heartbroken when I had to leave my pet cat behind in Toronto. To make matters worse, the landlord seems to be intent on eradicating cats in general.
Jason	Really? How so?
Melissa	Have you noticed the stray cats lurking about in alleys and in garages? There are a lot of stray cats in Seoul. I have seen very few Koreans who keep them as pets.

1. I'd much rather~
   I'd much rather have a cat.

2. Are you~ or~?
   Are you a cat person or a dog person?

3. This is such a~
   This is such a great pad you've got.

4. How did you manage to~?
   How did you manage to score such a nice place like this?

1

I'd much rather _____.

내 생각엔 _____ 하는 편이 더 좋겠어.

I'd much rather have a cat.

I'd rather~ 와 I'd rather not 두 가지를 배우겠습니다. "내 생각엔 ~하는 편이 더 좋겠어"라는 자기 의견을 밝힐 때 가장 유용한 표현이 되겠습니다. 물론 rather 뒤에는 동사 원형이 오고, '~하지 않는 편이 좋겠어'라면 not을 넣으면 되지요.

A. I'd rather + 동사 원형~: 제 생각엔 ~하는 편이 좋겠습니다.

   I'd much rather have a cat.
   저는 차라리 고양이를 기르겠어요.

I'd rather wait until tomorrow.

내일까지는 기다려보려고.

B. I'd rather + 동사 원형 + A than B : 제 생각엔 A하는 편이 B하는 것보다 좋겠습니다.

I'd rather stay home than go out with him.

그와 데이트를 하느니 차라리 집에 있을래요.

I'd rather marry than stay single.

독신으로 있는 것보다는 결혼하는 편이 낫겠어요.

C. I'd rather not + 동사 원형 ~ : 제 생각엔 ~하지 않는 편이 좋겠습니다.

I'd rather not spend money.

돈을 쓰지 않는 편이 좋을 것 같습니다.

I'd rather not make him upset.

그 남자를 화나게 하지 않는 편이 좋아.

2

Are you _____ or _____?

당신은 _____ 예요. 아니면 _____ 인가요?

Are you a cat person or a dog person?

Are you a cat person or a dog person?에는 두 가지 구문이 숨어 있습니다. 첫 번째는 are you A or B? 구문이고, 두 번째는 a 명사 + person으로 '~을 좋아하는 사람'이라는 구어적인 표현입니다. 특히 두 번째는 매우 쉬우면서도 자주 사용할 수 있는 표현입니다.

A. Are you A or B?: 당신은 A예요 아니면 B인가요?

Are you a cat person or a dog person? I'm a dog person myself.
당신은 고양이를 좋아해요, 개를 좋아해요? 저는 사실 개를 더 좋아하는데요.
Are you a morning person or a night owl?
아침형 인간이에요 아니면 밤에 주로 일을 하시는 편인가요?

B. a(n) 명사 + person: ~를 좋아하는 사람

I'm totally a bread person.
저는 빵을 너무 좋아해요.
She is absolutely a people person. She is very sociable.
그녀는 사람들하고 지내는 걸 참 좋아해요. 사회성이 좋은 거죠.

3

This is such a _____.   여기는 굉장한 _____ 입니다.
This is such a great pad you've got.

This is such a + 명사 구문입니다. 단순히 This is~ 명사였다면, '여기는 ~합니다' 라는 평범한 뜻일텐데, such라는 부사가 하나 들어가면서, 감탄문이 됩니다. such는 회화에서 주로 '매우, 대단하게, 그렇게' 등의 의미로 사용됩니다. 물론 앞 말을 받아서 '그렇게, 그러한'으로도 사용됩니다. 아예 'such a(n) + 형용사 + 명사' 어순을 외워서 사용하세요. 문법을 아는 것도 중요하지만, 일상 대화에서 쉽게 사용하려면, 즉각즉각 머리에서 그리고 입에서 나와야 합니다!

A. This is such a(n) + 형용사 + 명사: 여기는 굉장한 ~입니다.

This is such a great pad you've got. I love how you decorated it.
여기는 정말 멋진 곳인걸요. 당신이 꾸민 방식이 너무 맘에 들어요.

90

This is such a nice restaurant. Have you ever been here?

너무 멋진 식당이네요. 여기 오신 적 있어요?

B. such a(n) + 형용사 + 명사: 굉장한 ~

He has such a beautiful voice.

그는 정말 멋진 목소리를 가졌어요.

Where are you going in such a hurry?

도대체 어디를 그처럼 서둘러서 가시는 거예요?

4

How did you manage to _____?

어떻게 _____ 할 수 있었습니까?

How did you manage to score such a nice place like this?

How did you manage to + 동사 구문입니다. "어떻게 ~할 수 있었습니까?"라고 묻죠. How did you + 동사, 그리고 how do you + 동사 구문으로도 확대해볼 수 있습니다.

A. How did you manage to + 동사 구문?: 어떻게 ~할 수 있었습니까?

A: How did you manage to score such a nice place like this?

이렇게 멋진 곳을 어떻게 경제적으로 운영하실 수 있었나요?

B: The university helped me out.

대학이 도와주었습니다.

B. How did you + 동사 구문?: 어떻게 ~할 수 있었습니까?

How did you get such a nice place?

어떻게 이처럼 멋진 곳을 찾았어요?

How did you know about her pregnancy?
그녀의 임신에 대해서 어떻게 알게 됐어?

C. How do + 주어 + 동사 구문?: 어떻게 ~하나요?

How do I know that you are the one and only?
당신이 바로 그 사람인 걸 제가 어떻게 알 수 있나요?

How do we get to the subway station from here?
우리가 여기서 지하철역까지 어떻게 갈 수 있을까요?

Alternative Expressions

1

pad: slang for apartment
    digs
    crash pad
    crib
    joint
    haunt

2

a "creature of comfort" is someone who likes certain objects or amenities to make him or herself feel comfortable. It comes from the phrase, "creature comforts." This refers to the objects and things that make your life comfortable such as TV, computer, stereo system, furniture, technology, etc. Usually it is used in reference to one's home. Thus, there is the phrase, "the comforts of home."

3

It all worked out in the end.
= It all came together in the end.
= It all went smoothly in the end.
= It concluded very nicely.
= It ended well.

How did you manage to score such a nice place like this?

= How did you get such a nice place?

= How did you snag such a nice place?

= How did you find such a catch?

A cat person/dog person

A person who prefers cats/A person who prefers dogs

People person: a sociable person [see "social butterfly" in Chapter Two.]

To make matters worse~

= Even worse~

= What's even worse~

= Worse yet~

= Worse still~

= To add insult to injury~

1. 가구 찾으러 여기저기 다녔어요.
I had to scrounge around to find some of the furniture.

찾으러 다니는 것도 find, look for, look around 대신에 좀더 real and live다운 표현을 사용해봅시다.

- hunt around/all over
- poke around a bit
- do a little searching

2. 우리는 제법 잘 어울려요. We've got good chemistry.

"우리는 제법 잘 어울려요"는 제가 좋아하는 노래제목이기도 합니다. 성시경이 불렀죠. 여기 완벽한 영어표현이 있습니다. 원래 chemistry는 화학과목을 뜻합니다. 화학실험을 하면 각종 물질이 왜 섞이면서 잘되기도 하고, 안 되면 폭발하기도 하고, 다양한 반응을 일으키잖아요. 사람간의 변화, 마음의 움직임, 궁합 혹은 죽이 맞는다는 것 모두를 영어로는 chemistry로 표현합니다. 좀더 과장을 해서 하늘에서 맺어준 인연이라고 하면 또 어떨까요? "그들은 정말 환상의 커플이라고요."

- They've got great chemistry. I'm really happy for them.
- They are a match made in heaven.

Korea and Cats

Melissa   Cats are viewed more as pests or nuisances, kind of like rats or pigeons.

Jason   Interesting. I'm still new to Seoul so I guess I hadn't noticed. **Why do you suppose that is**?

Melissa   I'm not exactly sure. But I do know that many people consider them to be unsanitary or even bad luck. Plus, they always seem to be scavenging for food and creating a mess by tearing open the garbage bags in the street. So my landlord has even set out poisoned traps to kill them.

Jason   Come to think of it, I have noticed cats yowling at night and scurrying about in the parking garage of my friend's apartment. But I thought some cats were kept as pets.

Stella   Of course, some are. But cats have such a reputation for being independent and haughty, so I guess **they still haven't caught on** in Korea yet.

Melissa   **I never would have taken you to be** a cat person, Stella.

Stella   Oh really? Why do you say that?

Melissa   You're such an outgoing, friendly person. It just seems that a dog would suit your personality better. Dogs are friendlier. Cats seem so cold and antisocial.

Stella   That's a common perception, to be sure. I've met many people who are either afraid of cats or dislike them. But once you get to know them, it's a different story. Despite their reputation, cats can be quite affectionate!

Key Patterns

1. I never would have taken~
   I never would have taken you to be a cat person.

2. Once you get to know~
   Once you get to know them, it's a different story.

3. They still haven't caught on~
   They still haven't caught on in Korea yet.

4. Why do you~?
   Why do you suppose that is?

1

I never would have taken _____.

나라면 결코 _____ 하지 않았을 것이다.

I never would have taken you to be a cat person.

I (never) would have + 과거분사 구문입니다. 원칙적으로는 'would/could/ should/might + 동사의 과거분사형'은 가정법 문장의 주절에 사용됩니다. 그러나 if 절 없이도 많이 사용되기 때문에 구문의 형태를 우선 익혀두셔야 하고, 뜻도 '~했을 것이다(결코 ~하지 않았을 것이다)'로 정확히 이해하시기 바랍니다.

A. I would have + 과거분사~: 나라면 ~했을 것이다.

I would have done anything for you. You said no to me. You're making a big mistake, you know.
나는 너를 위해 무엇이든지 했을 거야. 나한테 아니라고 말하다니. 너 지금 큰 실수하는 거야!
I would have asked for her phone number.
나라면 그녀의 전화번호를 물어보았을 텐데.

B. I never would have + 과거분사~/I wouldn't have + 과거분사~: 나라면 ~ 결코 하지 않았을 것이다.

> **A: I never would have taken you to be a cat person, Stella.**
> 스텔라, 나는 정말 당신이 고양이를 좋아할 것이라고는 생각도 못했어요.
>
> **B: Oh really? Why do you say that?**
> 오, 정말요? 왜 그렇게 말씀하세요?

I wouldn't have done the same thing myself.
나라면 그렇게 똑같은 일을 하지는 않았을 거예요.

I would never get a headache from listening to loud music.
시끄러운 음악을 듣는다고 해서 머리가 아프거나 하지는 않을 거예요.

2

Once you get to know _____, 당신이 일단 _____ 알게 되면,
Once you get to know them, it's a different story.

Once you get to know + 명사 구문입니다. get to know는 시간을 들여서 알게 되는 것을 말합니다. Once는 '한번 ~한다면'의 뜻으로 사용되었습니다.

A. Once you get to know + 명사: 당신이 일단 ~ 알게 되면

Once you get to know them, it's a different story.
한번 알게 되면, 완전히 달라질걸.

Once you get to know me, you'll love me. Really.
당신이 저를 한번 알게 되면 저를 사랑하게 될 거예요. 진짜예요.

B. Once you + 동사 + 명사: 당신이 일단 ~하게 되면

Once you memorize the 26 letters of the alphabet, you'll be able to read English words.

일단 26개 알파벳을 외우고 나면, 당신은 영어 단어를 읽을 수 있습니다.

Once you meet my friends, you'll love them. They're awesome.

일단 내 친구를 만나고 나면, 그들을 좋아하게 될 거야. 내 친구들 멋지거든.

3

They still haven't caught on _____.

그들은 아직 _____ 에서 인기가 없어.

They still haven't caught on in Korea yet.

They still haven't caught on in Korea yet 문장에서 두 가지를 배우겠습니다. have + 과거분사형 구문으로 (1) 과거나 (2) 경험으로 사용된다는 것을 이미 알고 계실 테고요, catch on은 '~을 이해하다, 인기를 얻다, 유행하다' 는 뜻입니다.

A. have (not) + 과거분사: ~했다(~하지 않았다)

I have noticed cats yowling at night.

나는 밤에 우는 고양이들을 본 적이 있어요.

I have seen very few Korean who keep stray cats as pets.

저는 길 잃은 고양이를 애완동물로 기르는 한국인은 거의 본 적이 없어요.

B. catch on (to) (with) + 명사: ~을 이해하다, 인기를 얻다, 유행하다

So I guess they still haven't caught on in Korea yet.

내가 생각하기에는 아직 그들은 한국에서 인기가 없어.

Hip-hop has caught on throughout the world.

힙합음악이 전세계에서 인기를 얻고 있습니다.

Why do you _____? 당신은 왜 _____ 하십니까?
Why do you suppose that is?

Why do you suppose~?는 "당신은 왜 ~생각하십니까?"라는 뜻이지요. Why do you 다음에 다양한 동사를 넣어서 이유를 묻는 표현으로 사용합니다. 상대방의 의도나 목적이 궁금할 때, 친구나 동료 등 친한 사이에서 유용하죠.

A. Why do you suppose~?: 당신은 왜 ~생각하십니까?

> A: Cats are viewed more as pest or nuisances, kind of like rats or pigeons. 고양이는 들쥐나 비둘기처럼 좀 병균 취급을 받아요.
> B: Interesting. Why do you suppose that is?
> 흥미롭네요. 당신은 왜 그렇게 생각하시는데요?

B. Why do you + 동사~?: 당신은 왜 ~하십니까?

Why do you have to rush things? I think we have plenty of time.
당신은 왜 서두르시는 거죠? 우리에게 충분한 시간이 있다고 저는 생각하는데 말이죠.
Why do you think it's impossible?
당신은 왜 그것이 불가능하다고 하시나요?

Alternative Expressions

1

Come to think of it
= Now that you mention it
= Since you've said that~
= You know, that reminds me~

2

yowling
meowing - cats
mewing - kittens
barking - dogs
howling - dogs, wolves

3

scurrying about
= rushing about
= scuttling about
= scamper(ing) about

4

have [such] a reputation for~
= well-known for
= famous for
= noted for
notorious for [negative connotation]
feared for [negative connotation]

5

Once you get to know~

Once you try/taste/experience/see/hear~

~it's a(n) whole new ball game

    entirely different story

    completely different story

    whole new world

you'll never go back

Real & Live

1. 나는 말짱해요. I'm sober.

음주와 관련된 표현을 알아보겠습니다. 첫 번째는 술을 거의 마시지 않거나 전혀 마시지 않아서 정신적으로 말짱한 상태입니다. 당연히 I'm sober입니다. 다음은 약간 기분이 좋을 정도로 흔히 알딸딸하다고 표현할 만큼 음주를 한 경우가 됩니다. 그리고 다음 단계가 취했다는 정도이며 마지막은 술을 마시다가 흔히 black out이 될 만큼, 즉 필름이 끊기도록 심하게 마신 경우를 뜻합니다. 그래서 우리 끝까지 마셔보자는 영어 표현이 "Let's get wasted"가 되는 거죠.

- 저는 술 마시지 않았어요. 말짱합니다. I'm sober.
- 저는 좀 기분이 좋은데요. I'm buzzed.
- 술을 좀 많이 마셔서 취했습니다. I'm so drunk.
- 저는 너무 취해서 거의 죽을 것 같은데요. I'm so wasted.

2. 그는 술을 마시면 다 친구가 돼요. He's a friendly drunk.

- He's a(n) friendly/affectionate/quiet/talkative/angry drunk.

술에 대한 표현을 사람들의 버릇과 연관시켜보겠습니다. 사람들이 술을 마시고 나면 조금씩 변하는 경우가 있거든요. 어떻게 변하나요?

- 저는 다 친구가 돼요. I'm a friendly drunk.
- 그는 스킨십이 많아져요. 그렇죠? He's an affectionate drunk, isn't he?
- 당신은 말이 없어지시네요. You're a quiet drunk.
- 그녀는 말이 많아져요. She's a talkative drunk.
- 그 애들은 화를 내는 것 같더라. They're angry drunks.

In Praise of Cats

Jason	You don't find cats to be dirty scavengers who prowl around in garbage cans, eh?
Stella	Haha. **You'd be surprised**. Cats are actually quite clean. They groom themselves and unlike dogs, you don't have to pick up after them. It's only when they are homeless and starving that they become dirty.
Jason	Well, I don't even see many pet dogs in Seoul. There just doesn't seem to be enough space to walk them or take them outdoors.
Stella	Yes, that's why most pet dogs are smaller breeds. They are able to live in the smaller apartments here. Still, it's unfortunate that stray cats have such a bad reputation. They're even called *doduk goyangi*, which literally means "thief cats."
Melissa	I can relate to that. Still, cats give me the creeps. **I've never liked them**. **What is it that makes** cats so special for you, Stella?
Stella	I'm a sucker for their sense of independence. To me, dogs can be too co-dependent and overbearing. In contrast, cats can take care of themselves. In my opinion, they actually make the ideal house pet.

Melissa I disagree! Dogs are so cuddly, warm and affectionate. They give unconditional love. Cats are so stuck-up.

Stella More and more South Koreans would agree with you, Melissa. I see many women these days walking around with these very cute dogs. They are very pampered⋯sometimes with jewelry and dyed fur! I guess my personality just happens to prefer cats.

Melissa Well, **I'd still choose a dog over a cat any day**!

Key Patterns

1. I've never (liked)~
   I've never liked them.

2. You'd be surprised~
   You'd be surprised.

3. I'd still choose A over B.
   I'd still choose a dog over a cat any day!

4. What is it that makes~so special?
   What is that makes cats so special for you?

1

I've never (liked) _____ .   _____ 해본 적이 없습니다.
I've never liked them.

I've never (liked)~? 는 have + 과거분사를 이용한 현재완료 구문입니다. 회화를 잘하는 방법 가운데 한 가지는 단순한 현재동사나 과거동사를 사용한 문장보다, 현재의 경우 현재진행형 문장을, 과거형 문장의 경우 현재완료형을 잘 사용하는 것입니다. 각각 문장 자체를 현재와 연결시켜 좀더 생생한 표현으로 만들기 때문입니다.

쉽게 생각해보세요. I think of you, I thought of you보다는 I'm thinking of you, I've thought of you라고 하면 "지금 당신을 생각하고 있어요", "과거로부터 지금까지 쭉 생각하고 있어요"라는 감칠맛이 납니다. 단순히 문법이나 시제상의 문제라기보다는 생동감, 느낌을 다르게 한다는 것 잊지 마세요.

A. I have + 과거분사: ~해본 적이 있습니다.

> A: Have you ever been to America?
> 미국 가보신 적 있으세요?

B: No. I've only been to Japan.

아니요. 저는 일본만 가본 적이 있어요.

I have eaten a mango before when I was in Thailand.

태국에서 망고를 먹은 적이 있습니다.

Have you ever done anything illegal?

불법행위를 해본 적이 있으신가요?

B. I have + never + 과거분사: ~해본 적이 없습니다.

Cats give me the creeps. I've never liked them.

고양이는 여전히 좀 무서워요. 저는 결코 좋아한 적이 없어요.

I haven't decided to get engaged or married yet.

저는 약혼을 하거나 결혼을 해야겠다고 결심했던 적이 없어요.

2

You'd be surprised _____. 당신은 놀라실 거예요.
You'd be surprised.

You'd be surprised! "당신 놀라실
거예요"라는 뜻입니다. 이 구문에서
도 조동사 would를 사용하였습니다.
그리고 be surprised at처럼 한꺼
번에 외워야 하는 동사구를 몇 가지
살펴보도록 하겠습니다.

A. You would + 동사: 당신 ~하실
거예요.

You would be surprised. Cats are actually quite clean.

당신 놀라실걸요. 고양이들은 사실은 꽤 청결합니다.

You would be amazed at how beautifully she sings.

그녀가 얼마나 멋지게 노래를 하는지 당신은 아마 놀라시게 될 것입니다.

You would be satisfied with the quality of the workshop.

당신은 워크숍 수준에 대해서 만족하실 거예요.

She would be excited about making a new movie.

그녀는 새로운 영화를 찍는 데 흥분할 겁니다.

B. You would not + 동사: 당신 ~하지 못할 거예요.

You would not believe how he manipulated his crew.

그가 함께 일하는 사람들을 얼마나 악용했는지 당신은 아마 믿지 못하실 것입니다.

The boss would not trust her manager any more.

사장은 더 이상 그녀의 실무진을 신뢰하지 못할 것입니다.

3

I'd still choose A over B.   B 대신 A를 선택하겠습니다.
I'd still choose a dog over a cat any day!

I'd still choose A over B에서는 B 대신 A를 선택한다는 구문을 익히시면 됩니다.

A. choose/take A over B: B 대신에 A를 선택하다.

I'd still choose a dog over a cat any day.

저는 언제나 고양이보다는 강아지를 택할 거예요.

I'd take Dr. Yun's English Methodology class over Dr. Chung's Psychology 101.

정 선생님의 심리학 개론 수업보다는 윤 선생님의 영어 방법론 수업을 선택하겠습니다.

What is it that makes _____ so special?

_____를 대체 왜 그렇게 특별하게 생각하십니까?

What is that makes cats so special for you?

What is it that makes~so special? 문장을 그대로 번역한다면, "무엇이 ~를 특별하게 만듭니까?"라는 뜻이죠. "도대체 왜 그렇게 생각하느냐"는 상대방의 의견을 묻는 구문입니다.

A. What is it that makes~so special?: ~를 도대체 왜 그렇게 특별하게 생각하십니까?

What is it that makes cats so special for you?

당신에게 고양이는 왜 그렇게 특별한가요?

What is it that makes white shirts so special for you as a fashion designer?

패션 디자이너로서, 당신에게 흰 셔츠가 왜 그렇게 특별한가요?

Alternative Expressions

1

Pick up after

= clean up after your pet/dog

= pick up their feces

*Signs often say: "Please clean up after your dog."

2

There just doesn't seem to be enough [NOUN] to do something~

*always negative.

3

I can relate to that.

= I can see your point.

= I know what you're talking about.

= I agree.

= I know where you're coming from.

4

Give me the creeps

= give me the chills

= give me goosebumps

= give me the heebie-jeebies

= sends a chill up my spine

= [break out into a] cold sweat

5

stuck up
= arrogant
= cocky
= haughty
= full of oneself

6

still choose A over B
= I'd still choose A over B any day of the week.
= I'd take A over B.
= No contest.
= Not even a fair comparison.
= It's a no brainer.

1. 밀져야 본전이라고, 잃을 것도 없잖아! I've got nothing to lose.

"Enjoy the every moment in your life", "Carpe Diem" 모두 지금을 충실하게 살라는 표현입니다. 최근에 저는 Lipstick Jungle이라는 드라마의 한 장면에서 남자가 울고 있는 여자에게 "당신의 이야기는 모두 과거 시제로군요. 현재 시제에 좀더 관심을 가지세요"라며 위로하는 대사를 듣고 '아~' 하고 한동안 멍하게 있었습니다. 우리가 얼마나 자주 past tense를 사용하면서 후회를 하고 떨치지 못한 미련에 괴로워하는지 단박에 알 수 있잖아요. 지금, 이 순간을 사는 여러분의 대사에는 좀더 많은 present tense가 있어야 합니다. 우리 서로에게 약속!

- What do you have to lose?
- You have nothing to lose.
- It can't hurt to ask.
- Why not?
- Worth giving a shot.

2. 난 네게 반했어. I have a crush on you.

상대편에 대한 호감을 느끼는 것, 특히 이성적 관심을 갖게 되는 데 약 3초가 걸린다고 하네요. 상대편의 고백을 기다리다가 지치면 어떻하죠? 밴드 노 브레인(No Brain)의 노래처럼 아예 "넌 내게 반했어!" 이렇게 접근해볼까요?

- I have a crush on him.
- I've got such a crush on her.
- Do you have a crush on her?
- You have a crush on me, don't you?

Exercises

• Match-Up Words and Meaning

Words

Meaning

1. lurk •

• A. To enhance or make more attractive by adding ornaments, color, design, etc.

2. pamper •

• B. A situation that is difficult and which causes stress, anxiety and burdens

3. decorate •

• C. To wait secretly in hiding, usually because one intends to do something bad

4. hassle •

• D. To search among discarded waste or unwanted objects

5. reputation •

• E. The opinion that people have about oneself

6. scavenge •

• F. The characteristic of one who enjoys meeting and talking with people

7. outgoing •

• G. To lavish attention/care on a beloved object

Culture Corner

- Pets in the U.S.

Pets are immensely popular in America and the trend seems only to be increasing. Some statistics point out that there are more households that own pets than have children! According to an article in *USA Today*, 60 percent of all homes own a pet and more than two-thirds of these homes have more than one pet. While cats and dogs are the most popular pets, Americans are also known to keep birds, horses, reptiles, fish, and even exotic animals such as snakes and primates as pets.

As for the most popular pets, however, **cats and dogs** still remain on top. According to Wikipedia, there are more households that own dogs than cats, but the actual number of cats is higher (88 million) than the number of dogs (74 million). Thus, it is still a question of debate as to which is more popular.

The commonly perceived differences are notable between these two top runners. Cats are characterized as being solitary and independent. Unlike dogs, they seem content to keep to themselves, spending the entire day alone in an empty house. They are also viewed as self-sufficient since they clean themselves and use a litter box to go to the bathroom. Dogs, on the hand, seem to require as much love and attention as they give. Openly affectionate, they mingle and play well with humans and other dogs. Unlike the solitary nature of cats, dogs are also known for their "pack mentality." Though seen as friendlier and more social, dogs have to be "picked up after" and walked daily, and their barking can be quite boisterous! In general, dogs require much more attention and care from their owners than cats.

American **pet owners** express their love for their pets in a number of ways. According to statistics, Americans continue to spend a record amount each year in veterinary expenses, pet food and luxury toys and facilities. Some cats and dogs are known to be lavishly pampered by their adoring masters with pet clothing, spa treatments and hair salons! Nearly half of all pet owners consider their pets to be "members of the family." There are even pet cemeteries where owners can bury their loved ones. Clearly, Americans love their pets — whether they be cats, dogs or other!

Here are some expressions commonly used in American which indicate both positive and negative views toward cats and dogs:

dog eat dog world: a very cruel, brutal or competitive atmosphere or situation
call off the dogs: in the past, policemen used dogs to chase after criminals. Today it means to stop a strong verbal attack or criticism.
go to the dogs: a situation that is continually deteriorating or failing
dogs days of summer: the hottest days of summer
You can't teach an old dog new tricks.: It is difficult to teach someone who is stubbornly set in their ways by force of habit or custom.
tail wagging the dog: A situation where a small part is controlling the whole of something
work like a dog: To work slavishly or diligently
fat cat: A negative term that refers to someone very rich, spoiled and lazy
cat got your tongue: Words said to someone who is at a loss for words
curiosity killed the cat: An expression that means that it is not wise to be

too curious about a matter

"**fraidy cat**" **or** "**scaredy cat**": A taunt used by children to another child who is scared

Look what the cat dragged in!: Commonly, cats will kill mice, birds or some animal and then proudly bring it into the house. Thus, this is a humorous way to say, "Look who's here!"

cat and mouse: a situation of intrigue, cunning and pursuit

There's more than one way to skin a cat.: There is more than one way or method to do something.

When the cat's away, the mice will play.: when a person of authority (such as a boss or a teacher) is absent, subordinates can relax and feel free to engage in fun or mischief.

Business Matters

Lesson 11

Job Interview

Lesson 12

Business Meeting

Lesson 13

Business Problem

In Theme V, Alex is seen working at his corporate office setting. First, he interviews Eunji, a prospective employee who seeks an administrative post at his company. She is nervous about working for a large, international company under foreign management, but Alex is quick to reassure her not to feel pressured. In the next two lessons, Alex must deal with the impetuous business dealings of Noah, who makes unwise business choices. Despite having warned Noah about the risks inherent in a particular deal, Alex learns that Noah has gone ahead and made the deal with disastrous consequences. In the fallout, Alex and his other colleague Robert assess the damage and take steps to contain the problem.

Job Interview

Alex   Hi, Ms. Lee. I'm Alex Choi. Thanks for stopping by. I was just reviewing your resume. So far, everything looks quite good. So you just graduated from Korea National Open University?

Eunji   Yes, I received my B.A. in English last February.

Alex   And what have you been doing since then?

Eunji   I've been working part-time as an English teacher at a *hagweon* during the day and doing some private tutoring at night. It's a full schedule, but it keeps me busy!

Alex   Do you have any prior experience working as an administrative assistant?

Eunji   Well, **I used to** work as a part-time secretary at a small company in Yeouido, but I··· uh, I···

Alex   Yes? **You were saying**?

Eunji   I'm sorry, I'm just a little nervous. It's just that I've never worked for such a large and successful firm before. People told me not to bother even applying to such a prestigious company like this. I feel a little out of my league, to be honest.

Alex   Haha. **Who gave you that idea**? Please don't worry, Eunji. You're one of our final candidates and you seem perfectly qualified. In fact, I rather like your honesty! Please don't feel any pressure.

Eunji   Thank you, Mr. Choi. I feel more comfortable already. I really want you to know that I am a hard worker and I always put forth my best effort in whatever I do.

Alex   I'm sure you do. By the way, how good is your writing in English? **The position involves** a lot of writing in English and we're looking for somebody who can really handle a lot of e-mails and formal letters.

Eunji   I feel quite confident about my writing skills. As you can see from my resume, I studied at Australian National University for two years. My scores were very high on the writing portion of the TOEFL exam and I also have a lot of experience with writing letters in English.

Alex   Well, I've got to hand it to you, Eunji. I'm sold on your honesty and your earnestness. I really think you'll make a good fit with our team. When can you start?

Key Patterns

1. I used to~
   I used to work as a part-time secretary.

2. You were saying?   You were saying?

3. The position involves~
   The position involves a lot of writing.

4. Who gave you that idea~?   Who gave you that idea?

1

I used to _____ .

예전에 _____ 했었는데 지금은 더 이상 아니에요.

I used to work as a part-time secretary.

I used to~는 과거에 했던 일에 대해 이야기하는 구문입니다. "예전에 ~했었는데, 지금은 더 이상 아니에요"라는 뜻이 됩니다.

A. I used to + 동사 원형: 예전에 했던 일에 대해 더 이상 ~하지 않아요.

I used to work as a part-time secretary.
예전에 아르바이트로 비서로 일한 적이 있습니다.

He used to know how to speak Japanese but he forgot almost all of it after he came back to Korea.
그는 예전에는 일본어를 할 줄 알았는데, 한국에 돌아오고 나서 거의 다 잊어버렸어요.

B. I used to + 동사 원형: 과거 한때 예전의 상태에 대한 표현

I used to live in Vancouver, Canada.
캐나다 밴쿠버에 산 적이 있습니다.

A: You haven't changed at all!
너 하나도 안 변했구나!

B: Stop kidding me! I used to be hot but now I wear a size 77.
놀리지 마, 나 정말 한때 잘 나갔는데, 지금은 77 사이즈 입는다고.

2

You were saying _____?   당신 뭐라고 하는 거죠?
You were saying?

You were saying~?은 Are you saying (that)~?와 함께 알아둡니다. 상대편의 문장을 듣고 다시 묻거나, 확인을 하기 위해 다시 말해달라고 하는 거죠.

A.   You were saying~: 당신 뭐라고 하는 거죠?

A: I received my B.A. in English last February. But I…uh, I…
저는 지난 2월에 영어 학사 학위를 받았습니다. 그런데…

B: Yes? You were saying?
네? 뭐라고 말씀하셨어요?

A: I'm sorry. I'm just a little nervous.
죄송합니다. 제가 좀 긴장을 했습니다.

B.   Are you saying (that)~?: ~라는 말인가요?

Are you saying that we're doing the project together?
지금 우리가 함께 그 프로젝트를 진행한다는 말씀이신가요?

A: Are you saying that I have to look for another doctor?
다른 의사를 찾아봐야 한다고 제게 말씀하시는 거죠?

B: I'm not saying that he's a bad doctor. But he is not a specialist.

그가 나쁜 의사라는 말이 아니에요. 그저 그는 전문의가 아니라는 거죠.

3

The position involves _____.

이 직책은 _____ 할 의무가 있습니다.

The position involves a lot of writing.

The position involves~는 직업과 관련해서 유용하게 사용할 수 있는 구문입니다. Involve의 동사 뜻이 '관련하다, 포함하다'이니, position 자리에 다양한 명사를 넣어보시고, 동사 뒤에 목적어로도 여러 가지 명사를 넣어보세요. 그리고 be involved in, be involved with 등으로 확대시켜봅시다.

A. The position involves~: 이 직책은 ~할 의무가 있습니다.

A: The position involves a lot of writing and communicating in English.
이 직책은 영어로 글쓰기와 의사소통을 굉장히 많이 해야 합니다.

B: I feel quite confident about my writing skills.
저는 제 작문 실력에 대해서 자신감을 갖고 있어요.

To accept the appointment would involve living in Brisbane, Australia.
이 임명을 수락한다는 것은 오스트레일리아 브리즈번에서 살게 되는 것을 포함합니다.

B. be involved in, be involved with: ~에 연루되다, 연결되다.

Don't be involved in any trouble before you leave this country.
이 나라를 떠나기 전에 어떤 문제에도 말려들지 않도록 하세요.

I was involved in various projects with my co-workers.
제 동료들과 함께 다양한 분야에서 일했습니다.

4

Who gave you that idea _____?

누가 그런 생각을 하게 했나요?

Who gave you that idea?

Who gave you that idea?는 비슷한 표현으로 Where did you get that idea?, Who told you that? 등이 있습니다. 도대체 어떻게 그런 생각을 했냐는 질문이 되겠죠.

A. Who gave you that idea?: 누가 그런 생각을 하게 했나요?

> **A: People told me not to bother even applying to such a prestigious company like this.**
> 사람들이 이처럼 대단한 회사에는 서류도 내지 말라고 말했거든요.
>
> **B: Who gave you that idea?**
> 누가 그렇게 말했어요?

Where did you get that idea?
어디서 그런 생각을 했나요?

Who told you that?
누가 그렇게 하라고 말했어요?

Alternative Expressions

1

B.A. = Bachelor's degree = Bachelor of Arts (also, A.B.)
Bachelor of Science = B.S.
undergraduate degree

2

Master's degree
Master of Arts or Master of Science
M.A. or M.S.

3

Ph.D.
doctorate in~
M.D. for physicians.
J.D. for attorneys

4

part-time/full-time/temporary
in-house
on staff
paid staff
salaried
commission
working from home

5

a little out of my league

= a little beyond me~

= a little too advanced for me~

6

Please don't feel any pressure.

= take it easy.

= don't worry.

= Relax.

= Rest assured,~

7

I've got to hand it to you/him/her.

= I have to give you credit.

= I'm impressed.

= You did a good job.

8

I'm sold

= I'm sold on [someone or something.]

= I'm convinced of the value of [someone or something.]

= I'm convinced!

= I'm sold on Samsung TVs!

= I admit, you've won me over!

Real & Live

1. 그는 원칙을 어기고 있어요. He's breaking all the rules.

좀 오래된 노래 Torn between two lovers에는 "Torn between two lovers, feeling like a fool. Loving both of you is breaking all the rules."라는 가사가 나옵니다. 두 남자 사이에서 갈등하는 여자의 노래인데, 두 사람 을 다 사랑한다는 것은. 한마디로 원칙에서 벗어난다는 겁니다. '규율을 어겼다, 규칙 위반이다 혹은 원칙에서 벗어난다' 는 것을 다양한 표현으로 배워보겠습니다. 이 표현은 일터, 비즈니스 상황 에서 적절하게 사용할 수 있는 매우 유용한 표현입니다.

- bending the rules
- tweaking the rules
- playing with the rules
- skirting with the law

2. "우리"를 중시한다고. I'm a team player.

개인적인 것과 이기적인 것은 매우 다릅니다. Individual한 것은 사실 굉장히 긍정적인 것으로 자신의 시공간을 지키기 위해 그만큼 혹은 그 이상 타인의 시공간을 배려한다는 것을 전제로 합니다. 그러나 selfish한 것은 타인에 대한 배려 없이 모든 것을 자기만을 위해 생각하고 행동하는 것이니 배타적이지요. 우리가 혼자서는 살아갈 수 없는 "사회" 에 살고 있다고 한다면 그만큼 team으로 일하는 기회가 많겠습니다. 자신의 일을 남에 게 미루지 않고, 서로서로 도와간다면 최상이겠고요.

- I run a very tight ship at this company, but I am also a team player. And we're all on the same team!
  내가 지금 회사를 완전히 장악하고 있긴 하지만, 그래도 나 역시 우리를 중시하는 사람입니다. 우리 모두는 같은 팀이라고요.

Business Meeting

Alex   Thanks for coming on such short notice, Noah. We need to talk about this new plan to buy the property on Yeoido. **I have decided** that we should buy the land later when prices drop.

Noah   May I offer a minority view?

Alex   Go ahead. Tell me what's on your mind.

Noah   I know that you and the board of directors want to proceed with caution, but I strongly disagree. Prices will only get higher. I'd say that it's likely that if we don't buy right now, we **will miss out**.

Alex   **What about** the fact that there are warning signs that prices are too high and that the real estate bubble is going to burst?

Noah   With all due respect, Alex, you're too timid. I'm willing to bet that prices won't take a major nosedive anytime soon. We can't go wrong.

Alex   You're missing something, Noah. The market can't possibly go on like this. Have you ever considered the possibility that things might go bust?

Noah   In my view, the price of land can continue indefinitely. We would save a lot of money if we go all in and bet the farm now.

Alex   It would be unwise to make such a rash decision. If you want to buy, then go ahead, but I'm not going to be a party to it. I will officially oppose your plan if you present it to the board.

Noah   No, **you've got it all wrong**, Alex. I can assure you that my analysis is spot on. I've crunched the numbers over and over again and my conclusion is solid.

Alex   We shall see.

Key Patterns

1. I have decided~
   I have decided that we should buy the land later.

2. You've got it all wrong~   You've got it all wrong.

3. We'll miss out~   We'll miss out.

4. What about~?
   What about the fact that there are warning signs that prices are too high and the real estate bubble is going to burst?

1

I have decided _____.   _____ 하기로 결정했습니다.

I have decided that we should buy the land later.

I have decided that we should buy the land later에서는 I have decided that~ 구문을 배워봅시다. 이미 그렇게 결정했다는 거죠.

A. I have decided (that)~ : ~하기로 결정했습니다.

> A: I have decided that we should buy the land later when prices drop.
> 가격이 내려갈 때 그 토지를 구매하기로 결정했습니다.
>
> B: May I offer a minority view?
> 제 소견을 말씀드려도 될까요?

I have decided to go back to the U.S.
미국으로 되돌아가기로 결정했습니다.

I have decided not to tell him the truth.
나는 그에게 진심을 말하지 않기로 했어요.

B. I've + 과거분사형 (that)~: 과거로부터 지금까지 ~하고 있습니다.

I've heard that you tried to move out from your place.
당신이 이사하려고 한다는 이야기를 듣고 있었어요.

I've had a hard time these days. It was really tough.
요즘 계속 좀 힘들었어요. 진짜 힘들더라고요.

This is the best grade that I've ever gotten.
제가 받은 최고 성적이에요.

2

You've got it all wrong _____.

당신은 완전히 틀렸어요.

You've got it all wrong.

You've got it all wrong~은 두 가지로 나누겠습니다. wrong에 해당하는 표현을
다양하게 바꿔서 알아보고요, You've got to~를 배워봅니다.

A. You've got it (all) + 형용사~: 당신은 완전히 ~했어요.

You've got it all wrong. 당신 완전히 틀렸어요.
You've got it all mixed up. 당신 완전히 헷갈리고 있는 거예요.
You've got it backwards. 거꾸로 이해하셨습니다.
You've got it right. 맞았어요. 바로 그 말이에요.

B. You've got to + 동사 원형: 지금 이 시점에서 해야 할 일은 ~입니다.

You've got to understand the manual.
사용설명서를 이해하셔야지요.

You've got to put on some sunscreen cream.
지금 자외선 차단제를 바르셔야 합니다.

3

We'll miss out _____ .   우리는 기회를 놓치게 될 겁니다.

We'll miss out.

We'll miss out. 평서문에서는 miss out의 뜻을 이해하고, 과거형과 미래형 시제로 다양하게 연습해보겠습니다.

A. We missed out~ : 우리는 기회를 놓쳤어요.

We missed the boat.
그들은 보트를 놓쳤습니다.

We missed (=lost) our chance.
우리는 기회를 놓친 거죠.

B. We'll miss out~ : 우리는 기회를 놓치게 될 것입니다.

If we don't buy right now, we will miss out.
우리가 지금 구입하지 않으면 기회를 놓치게 됩니다.

You'll miss your chance.
당신은 기회를 놓칠 겁니다.

4

What about _____ ?   _____ 는 어때요?

What about the fact that there are warning signs that prices are too high and the real estate bubble is going to burst?

What about~?은 제안을 할 때 가장 잘 사용하는 표현입니다. 시간이나 장소를 제안할 때, 혹은 어떤 사람에 대해서 묻거나 일이 잘 진행되고 있는지 물어볼 때도 사용할 수 있습니다. 특히 잊으면 안 되는 일을 꼭 집어 말할 때 유용하죠.

How about~?과 혼용하는 경우가 있습니다만, 정확하게 말하자면 What about~?
은 What about your exam next Saturday?처럼 보다 중요한 일인 경우가 있습니
다. 그리고 How about~?은 친한 사람끼리 권유나 의견을 묻는 경우에 주로 사용합
니다. How about going to the movies tonight? 혹시 구분하실 수 있을까요?

A. What about~?: ~는 어쩌죠?, ~는 어때요?, ~는 어떻게 되었나요?

What about the fact that real estate prices have continued to skyrocket over the past two years?
지난 2년간 부동산 가격이 끊임없이 오른 사실은 어떻습니까?

What about "Love Actually" instead of "Notting Hill"?
노팅힐보다는 러브 액츄얼리를 보는 것이 어떨까?

What about next Friday?
다음 주 금요일은 어때요?

B. How about~?: ~은 어떨까요?

How about a nice Virgin Pina Colada?
무알콜 피나콜라다 한 잔 어때요?

How about a better attitude?
태도를 좀 얌전히 하시지요.

Alternative Expressions

1

prices drop
= fall
= decline
= go down
= lower

2

You will miss out.

Future:	You will miss out.	Past:	You missed out.
Future:	You'll lose your chance.	Past:	You lost your chance.
Future:	You'll miss your chance.	Past:	You missed your chance.
Other:	You missed the boat.		
	You lost out.		

3

"all in" and "bet the farm"

= you are risking everything

*To spend all the money you have because you feel something is worth the risk.

4

I'm not going to be a party to it.

= I want no part of this.
= I will not go along with this.
= Count me out.

5

spot on

= exactly right
= on the money

1. 꽝이야! Go bust!

한국어로도 실패했다는 것과 꽝이라는 느낌이 좀 다르지요? go bust는 fail 했다는 뜻입니다. 좀더 쉽게는 타이어가 펑크가 나거나 풍선이 터지는 것을 상상하시면 돼요.

● Is there any possibility that things might go bust?
   일이 실패할 가능성이 있습니까?

남쪽으로 가는 것이 왜 실패를 뜻하게 되었는지는 설이 분분합니다만, 어쨌든 실패한다는 뜻이며, 최악의 상황이 된다는 것, 면전에서 폭발이 일어나거나 뒤집어진다는 것, 결국은 다 '실패한다, 꽝이다' 라는 것입니다. 이해하실 수 있죠?

● go South
● take a turn for the worst
● explode in one's face
● flop

2. 열두 시 반 정도에 만나뵙는 걸로 하지요. Let's meet at 12:30ish.

시간 약속을 할 때 우리가 늘 정각에만 만나자고 할 수 없잖아요. 몇 시쯤 혹은 대충 그때 정도라고 하고 싶으면 영어로는 어떻게 할까요? 아주 쉽습니다. 시간과 상황 뒤에 ~ish라는 어미를 붙이세요.

- 여섯 시쯤은 어떨까? How about meeting at 6ish?
- 정오 정도에 들러보도록 할게. I'll try to stop by around noonish.

만약 12시 정각도 부족해서 절대 서로 늦지 않고 정확한 바로 그 시간에 만나자고 하면 뒤에 sharp라는 표현을 넣으시면 됩니다.

- 3시 정각이야, 알았지? 3 o'clock, sharp, ok?
- 12시 정각에 만나는 거야. 약속 늦지 말고! Let's meet at noon, sharp!

Business Problem

Alex   Robert, what happened to the Yeouido property? It's a disaster!

Robert   Sorry, Alex. It's way over budget and as you predicted, the market just crashed and burned. Now the property is worthless. In hindsight, Noah was foolish to put all his eggs in one basket. The deal is a complete washout.

Alex   Oh, great. And now we're left holding the bag. Now **we have no choice but to** clean up this mess.

Robert   I would have thought Noah would let the board know before making his move.

Alex   No dice. Noah should have just cooled his heels when he got the authority to make purchases, but he rushed into the purchase without thinking.

Robert   Even worse, it turns out that Noah never even thought to factor in the cost of complying with new environmental regulations. His budget is now much higher than he originally estimated.

Alex   You have got to be kidding me. **Whatever happened to** accountability?

Robert   We may just have to cut our losses and move on.

Alex   Unbelievable. **Can you believe** how much money this is going to cost us? We're really in a jam now.

Robert   I think we may be able to explore the possibility of re-selling the property in Yeoido to an outside investor. But we would need outside help. Would you like for me to go ahead and hire a consultant?

Alex   At this point, **I don't see why not**. Let him name his price and just sign the contract. We need him as soon as possible. We'll hammer out the details later.

Key Patterns

1. I don't see why not~   *I don't see why not.*

2. Can you believe~?
   Can you believe how much money this is going to cost us?

3. We have no choice but to~
   We have no choice but to clean up this mess.

4. Whatever happened to~?
   Whatever happened to accountability?

1

I don't see why not _____.   왜 안 되는지 잘 모르겠습니다.
I don't see why not.

I don't see why not은 문장을 통으로 외우세요. I don't see에서 see가 '보다' 라는 뜻이 아니라 '이해하다' 라는 것은 알고 계시죠? 안 되는 이유가 없다는 뜻입니다. 다음 단계는 see의 자리에 know, think, want, get을 넣어서 표현을 다양하게 만드는 거죠.

A. I don't see why not.: 왜 안 되는지 잘 모르겠습니다.

　A: Would you like for me to go ahead and hire a consultant who can help us?
　　그럼 우리를 도울 수 있을 만한 컨설턴트를 채용하도록 할까요?

　B: Hmmm. I don't see why not.
　　음. 그렇게 하지 않을 이유가 없죠.

　I don't see why Jim didn't call me.
　짐이 왜 내게 전화하지 않는지 모르겠어.

I don't see how she maintains her Chinese even after she came back home. 그녀가 고국으로 돌아온 이후에도 어떻게 그렇게 중국어를 유지하는지 궁금해.

B. I don't + 동사(know, think, want, get): ~하지 않아요.

I don't know what to do now.
무엇을 해야 할지 모르겠습니다.

I don't think we were friends.
우리가 친구였다고 생각하지 않아요.

I don't want you to eat French fries and a hamburger tonight.
오늘은 감자튀김과 햄버거를 먹고 싶지 않아.

2

Can you believe _____? _____을 믿을 수 있나요?

Can you believe how much money this is going to cost us?

Can you believe~? 역시 위의 1번처럼 can you believe~?를 익히는 것이 첫 단계입니다. 믿기지 않는 사실에 대해서 믿을 수 있냐고 묻는 뜻이며, 명사나 that절 이 뒤에 옵니다. 그리고 can you + 동사~?로 다양하게 배워보겠습니다.

A. Can you believe + 명사?, Can you believe (that)~?: ~을 믿을 수 있어요?

A: Can you believe how much money this is going to cost us?
우리가 얼마나 지불해야 하는지 믿을 수 있습니까?

B: I think we may be able to explore the possibility of re-selling the property.
그 건물을 되팔 가능성에 대해서 생각해볼 수 있을 것 같 습니다.

₩9,000,000,000

Can you believe what the teacher said?

선생님이 뭐라고 했는지 믿을 수 있겠어?

Can you believe Helen is dating that cute guy?

헬렌이 저렇게 멋진 남자랑 사귄다는 것을 믿을 수 있어?

B. Can you + 동사 + 명사? Can you + 동사 (that + 절)~?: ~할 수 있어요?

Can you tell me when the club opens?

클럽이 언제 여는지 알려주실래요?

Can you do me a favor?

저 좀 도와주시겠어요?

Can you get her cell phone number?

그녀 핸드폰 번호 알아다 줄 수 있지?

3

We have no choice but to _____ .

_____ 하는 것 외에는 다른 방법은 없습니다.

We have no choice but to clean up this mess.

We have no choice but to~은 "~하는 것 외에는 다른 방법은 없습니다"라는 뜻입니다. No choice but to가 핵심 구문이죠. but을 늘 "그러나"로만 알고 있는 사람들이 있습니다. 그러나 but의 중요한 뜻 중 하나가 "~을 제외하고"라는 거 아시죠? 이 구문의 의미와 함께 but 다음에 to 부정사가 온다는 것도 기억하세요.

A. no choice but to~: ~할 수밖에 없다, ~외에 다른 선택은 없다.

We have no choice but to clean up this mess.

우리는 이 혼란을 말끔히 처리하는 것 외에는 다른 방법이 없습니다.

I have no choice but to say good-bye to him.

나는 그에게 이별을 고하는 것 외에는 다른 방법이 없어요.

The kids have no choice but to obey their parents.

그 아이들은 자신의 부모님을 따르는 것 외에는 다른 선택이 전혀 없을 것이다.

Whatever happened to _____?

_____ 일이 일어나다.

Whatever happened to accountability?

Whatever happened to~?는 what happened to~? 그리고 what happen to ~?까지 확대시켜 배워봅니다. 도대체 무슨 일이 일어났느냐는 느낌을 잘 살리세요. happen to가 우연하게 일어나는 일이라는 뜻이 가장 강하거든요. 문법적으로는 to 다음에 동사 원형이 오는 경우, 그리고 명사가 오는 경우가 있습니다.

A. Whatever happened to + 명사?/ what happened to + 명사?: ~일이 일어나다.

Whatever happened to accountability?
책임소재는 어떻게 되는 겁니까?

What happened to that little girl?
그 소녀에게 무슨 일이 있었습니까?

B. happen to + 동사 원형: 우연하게 ~하다.

Do you happen to know what time it is?
혹시 지금 몇 시인지 아세요?

I happen to know her email address. Do you need it?
내가 우연히 그녀의 이메일 주소를 알게 됐어. 혹시 필요해?

Alternative Expressions

1

"crashed and burned"

When something fails completely, we have a variety of expressions to vividly describe the disappointing situation:

flop (usually refers to a planned event such as a movie or play)

disaster

fiasco

2

washout

= a complete failure

dud

= refers to a grenade that fails to explode; when expectations are high but the results are a complete failure

E.g., We had hoped that the video would work, but it was a complete dud.

to crash and burn

= like an airplane that is shot out of the sky

E.g., I tried to ask Cindy out but I crashed and burned. She totally rejected me!

3

left holding the bag

To be left with someone else's responsibility. Literally, when a thief or robber escapes but his accomplice is caught or arrested. The second caught thief is "left holding the bag."

4

cooled his heels

= Take[n] it easy   = Take[n] it slow

= tread carefully   = proceeded cautiously

5

got to be kidding me

= You've got to be joking.

= You can't be serious.

= This must be a joke?

= Are you for real?

= This can't be for real!

= Are you pulling my leg?

= No way!

6

cut losses

This expression perhaps comes from the idea that you have to "cut" or sever your connection or line to things that are dragging you down. For example, if you are losing money or time, you may have to sacrifice that thing.

7

hammer out the details later

= work out the details later

= smooth out the details later

= iron out the details later

= smooth out the rough edges later

1. 모든 것을 걸었어요. I have all my eggs in one basket.

바구니 하나에 자신이 갖고 있는 달걀을 다 넣었다고 가정합니다. 혹시나 바구니를 떨어뜨리게 되면 다 깨지겠지요. 그래서 나온 표현입니다. 자신이 가진 모든 것을 한 방에 거는 것을 말합니다. 한꺼번에 모든 위험을 감수하는 것보다는 가능하다면 위험을 여러 곳에 분산시키는 것이 좋을 것이라는 권고로, 주로 속담처럼 많이 사용하는 표현도 함께 알아보겠습니다.

- 위험을 분산시키세요. Don't put all your eggs in one basket.
- 그는 이 사업에 모든 것을 걸었습니다. He put all his eggs in one basket.
- 그들의 계획이 예상이 빗나갔어요. They brought their eggs to a bad market.

2. 전혀 말이 안 돼. It is without rhyme or reason.

It doesn't make sense를 좀더 다양하게 활용해보겠습니다. rhyme이 운율이고 reason이 이유니까, It's is without rhyme or reason이라면 운율도 안 맞고, 이유도 없고, 결국 이리저리 아무리 노력해도 도무지 이해가 되지 않는다는 표현이 됩니다.

- It makes little sense.
- It makes little order.
- It is unreasonable.

Exercises

• Crossword Puzzle

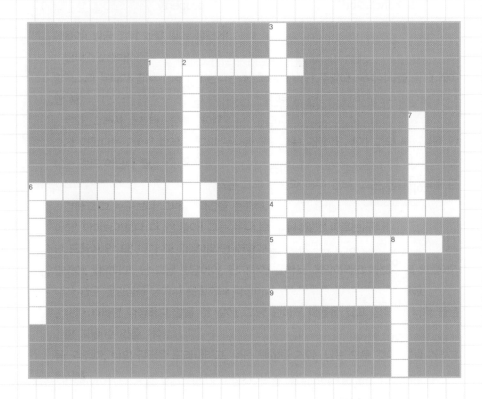

Across

1. A person who is employed to do office work, such as typing letters, answering phone calls, and scheduling meetings.
4. Being very serious and sincere in what one says or does because one thinks that one's actions and beliefs are important.

5. To decide that something is true after you have thought about it carefully and have considered all the relevant facts.
6. The likelihood or probability that something might happen.
9. That which can be depended upon to work well or to behave in a way that is consistent.

Down
2. Someone who is being considered for a position, for example someone who is running in an election or applying for a job.
3. The writing and exchange of letters to someone.
6. Material things or land that belongs to someone.
7. A large area of land which is owned by a person, family, or organization.
8. A person or group that buys shares of stocks in order to receive a return profit at a later date.

Culture Corner

- Resume and Interview Tips

Resume Tips

(a) List your **name**, **address** and **contact information** at the top. In the U.S., one does not need to reveal one's date of birth nor include a photograph. Such information in the United States would be considered grounds for age bias or discrimination.

(b) List a brief **summary of your skills**. These can be two or three bullet points. Keep this section short. You do not have to use complete sentences.

(c) Always be sure to align the content of your resume with the left margin. All content should be properly aligned.

(d) For your **educational or academic background**, list the academic institution, the degree you received (B.A., M.A., etc.) and the year you received your degree. Usually, you should begin with your college degree. If not, then list your high school degree.

(e) For your **work or professional experience**, make sure to list the **title of your position** and the **name of your place of employment**.

(f) Always include the **location** and **the date**. For example, "Seoul, S. Korea, 1999-2001."

(g) When giving a description of your work, you can drop the "I" personal pronoun and give a very succinct, professional account by starting with the VERB in the past tense.

(h) Note any **awards**, **scholarships**, **languages**, **interests** and/or **hobbies**.

(i) **References** are optional. If you do wish to cite your references, simply list the person's name, title and contact information. Make sure you address the reference person with "Mr.", "Ms." or the appropriate title before their formal (last) name.

Lance Kim

Jongno-gu, Dongsung-dong 199-8
SoHo B/D 101-ho
Seoul, South Korea
012-3456-7891
lancekim@email.com

(a)

SUMMARY OF SKILLS **(c)**

- Experienced English instructor with excellent interpersonal and communication skills
- Extensive background in teaching English as a Second Language (ESL) at elementary and high school levels

(b)

EDUCATION

University of Illinois Urbana-Champaign, Urbana-Champaign, IL
Master of Arts in Teaching of English as a Second Language (MATESL), August 2002

(d)

Korea National Open University, Seoul, S. Korea
Bachelor of Arts (English), May 1998

PROFESSIONAL EXPERIENCE

English Instructor, February 2008 - present
Premier English Academy, Seoul, S. Korea
Taught elementary/high school conversational English

(f) **(e)**

Writing Instructor, October 2003 - December 2007
Swift Hagweon, Seoul, S. Korea
Taught 10-week intensive writing programs to adult students.

Teaching Assistant, 2001-2002
University of Illinois Division of English as an International Language (DEIL) Program, Urbana-Champaign, IL
Assisted various professors in moderating class discussions and the grading of papers and exams. Duties included holding office hours and individual counseling for undergraduate students.

(g)

AWARDS

Student of the Year Award, DEIL Program, Univ. of Illinois, 2002
Phi Kappa Phi Scholarship Award Winner, 2001

(h)

ASSOCIATIONS

Korean Students Association, Vice-President 2002

LANGUAGES

Korean, English, French

HOBBIES/ INTERESTS

Judo, Cycling, Hiking

REFERENCES

Available upon request

(i)

Commonly Asked Interview Questions

Please tell us a little about yourself.

When did you leave your last job? Why?

Do you have any previous experience? OR Tell us about your prior work experience.

What would you say are your strengths? Your weaknesses?

Why do you think that you are qualified for this job?

What do you think you could contribute to this job?

What made you interested in applying for this position?

Why should we hire you?

Describe your work ethic.

Theme VI

Music and Words

Lesson 14

Musical Director

Lesson 15

Talk Show

In Theme VI, Michael is in the beginning stages of directing a new play and has a meeting with his new musical director, Terry. As director, Michael asks Terry to compose some musical pieces to provide background to his play, but gives great creative freedom for Terry to experiment. Terry reassures Michael that he can come up with a few options, but clarifies the timeline so as to remain on schedule. In the final lesson, Stella and her good friend Roy discuss the publication of their first book on a TV talk show in Seoul. The show is conducted in English, and Stella and Roy discuss their backgrounds and how they came to write this book, which is about their cultural observations as outsiders to Seoul.

Musical Director

Terry	So, what are we looking at here?
Michael	We need background music to several key scenes. These will be critical to the overall feel of the play and ultimately to its success. I really hope you have some ideas.
Terry	I have a few things kicking around upstairs. But let me know what you're after. It'll give me a clearer picture of what I should be aiming for.
Michael	We need something to fit with the setting which is set in the 1930s. I'd like you to experiment a bit with something classical or jazz.
Terry	**I imagine** that it shouldn't be too hard. If you give me a few days, I can come up with a **few things that might go with** that. How soon do you need it?
Michael	I'm in no rush. Does a week sound reasonable to you? Just give me a couple of musical options and we'll go from there.
Terry	No problem. You seem to like things spontaneous and free. **As long as you walk me** through the script we can play it by ear.

Michael You hit the nail on the head. I'm a hands-off director and I like to hear other people's ideas. Just go with the flow, you know what I mean?

Terry Sure, I'm cool with that. But **when is the latest** you need it by?

Michael If we haven't gotten anything done by say, the 25th, we're in trouble. We'd better get a move on by next month at the latest.

Terry That's plenty of time. I'll get back to you by this weekend and we should be good to go.

Michael Good! Let's call it a day. We've done enough work for today!

Key Patterns

1. I imagine that~
   I imagine that it shouldn't be too hard.

2. As long as you~
   As long as you walk me through the script together, we can play it by ear.

3. A (a few things) go/es with B.
   I can come up with a few things that might go with that.

4. When is the latest~?
   When is the latest you need it by?

1

I imagine that _____.   _____라고 상상하다, 생각하다.

I imagine it shouldn't be too hard.

I imagine that~은 쉬운 표현이죠? that 다음에 주어 + 동사 절을 만들어서 '~상상하다, ~생각하다' 고 하시면 됩니다. 자신의 의견을 구체적으로 개진한다고 생각하세요.

A. I imagine that + 주어 + 동사: ~라고 상상하다, 생각하다.

I imagine it shouldn't be too hard.
그렇게 어렵지는 않을 것이라고 기대합니다.

I imagine too many instruments would muddy the effect.
제 생각에는 너무 많은 악기를 사용하면 오히려 효과를 약화시킬 것 같아요.

As long as you _____. _____라면, _____인 이상

As long as you walk me through the script, we can play it by ear.

As long as~가 핵심 구문입니다. 접속사로 사용되어서 주어와 동사가 뒤에 오게 되며 '~라면, ~인 이상'이라는 뜻으로 해석합니다. 물론 as A as B와 같은 비교의 뜻이 있기도 하지요.

A. As long as + 주어 + 동사: ~하는 한 ~하다.

As long as you walk me through the script together, we can play it by ear.

우리가 함께 스크립트를 짚어나가면 그냥 들으면서도 연주를 할 수 있겠습니다.

You can work here with us as long as you want.

당신은 원하는 한 여기서 우리와 함께 일하실 수 있습니다.

As long as you don't get it off your chest, I can't help you out at all.

당신이 솔직하게 이야기하지 않는 이상, 제가 도울 수 있는 것은 없습니다.

B. As A as B: B만큼 A하다.

I just want to go home as soon as possible.

저는 될 수 있으면 빨리 집으로 돌아가고 싶어요.

I'm not as easy as you seem to think.

저는 당신이 생각하는 만큼 쉬운 사람 아니에요.

3

A (a few things) go/es with B.

A와 B가 잘 어울린다.

I can come up with a few things that might go with that.

A goes with B~가 핵심 구문입니다. A와 B가 잘 어울린다는 뜻이죠. 옷이나 사람 등 다양하게 사용할 수 있는 표현입니다. '동의하다, 동행하다, 교제하다' 등 여러 가지 문장을 같이 살펴봅니다.

A. A goes with B~ : A와 B가 잘 어울린다.

I can come up with a few things that might go with that.
그것과 잘 어울릴 만한 것을 몇 가지 제가 생각해낼 수 있겠는데요.

This land goes with the house with the white picket fence.
이 토지는 흰색 울타리 부잣집에 딸려 있습니다.

Your brooch goes well with the dress.
당신이 한 브로치가 옷과 정말 잘 어울립니다.

When is the latest _____? 가장 최후로 언제까지요?
When is the latest you need it by?

When is the latest~? 역시 when으로 시작하는 걸 보니 시간을 물어보는 표현이죠. 가장 늦게 언제까지인지 흔히 말하는 due, 마감 시간을 묻는 구문으로 외워두세요. 반대로 earliest~를 사용하면 어떤 뜻이 될까요?

그리고 특히 late-later-latest, late-latter-last 두 가지 종류의 비교급을 구분해서, 시간상으로 늦은 것인지, 순서상으로 늦는 것인지 확실히 하시기 바랍니다.

A. When is the latest~?: 가장 최후로 언제까지요?

When is the latest you need it by?
언제까지 그것이 필요하신가요?
When is the earliest you could finish the assignment?
당신이 가장 빨리 과제를 끝낼 수 있는 시기는 언제입니까?

B. When was the last time~?: 가장 마지막으로 ~한 게 언제입니까?

When was the last time you made a presentation and gave a report?
마지막으로 발표를 하시고 과제 보고를 한 것이 언제인가요?
When was the last time we went to the amusement park?
우리가 놀이공원을 간 것이 언제가 마지막이야?

Alternative Expressions

1

I have a few things kicking around upstairs.
kick around = to think about; ponder
upstairs = one's mind or brain
Meaning: to have some ideas

2

We will go from there.
= We will take it from there.
= We will start at that point.
= We will begin at that point.
= We will take over from there.

3

Walk me through~
Go through [this] with me
Take me through the process~
Please go step by step through the process~
Let's go through this together~

4

We can play it by ear.
= go with the flow
= We can decide then.
= We can worry about it later.
= We can think of something later.

5

We'd better get a move on~
= We'd better start leaving.
= We'd better hurry.
= It's time to get going.
= We should be leaving.
= We should be going.

6

good to go
means that everything is set or ready. All preparations have been made
and everything has been settled.

1. 오늘은 이만 하지. Let's call it a day.

해가 뜨면 일을 시작하고 해가 지면 일을 마쳤던, 그래서 낮을 하루라고 여기던 시절이 있었습니다. 요즘에야 24시간 일하는 경우도 많고, 야근까지 생각하면 밤낮없이 일을 하니까, day의 개념이 좀 달라졌지만요. 그래서 밤낮 개념과 관계없는 요즈음에도 "오늘 일은 여기서 끝냅시다, 퇴근합시다"는 예전에 그러했듯이 "이만큼의 낮을 하루라고 부르자"는 표현으로 굳었답니다.

- Let's stop here.
- Let's finish here.
- Let's wrap it up here.

2. 당신이 저랑 천천히 단계를 밟으면, 저는 할 수 있습니다.
If you walk me through it, I can do that.

한 가지씩 단계별로 과정을 거친다는 표현입니다. walk me through라고 함께 나란히 걷는 것을 상상하시면 됩니다. 걷는 것은 뛰거나 자동차를 타는 것과는 달리 속도를 내는 것에 한계가 있고, through라는 전치사가 과정을 건너뛰지 않고 그대로 따라간다는 느낌을 전합니다. 쉽게 go through, go step by step이라는 표현을 주로 사용합니다만, 보다 시적인 walk me through를 적절히 사용해보세요.

- Let's go through (this) together.
- Please take me through the process.
- Please go step by step through the process.

Talk Show

Host	Good morning everyone and welcome to another edition of "Talk Seoul." **You're in for a** treat today! For today's show, we have two very special guests. Stella Kingston is an English professor who has been teaching in Seoul for the past five years. Roy Park, also an English instructor, teaches at a foreign language high school. Together, they have just written a book titled, "Seoul: A Land of Contradictions." Thank you both for joining us.
Stella	Thank you for having us.
Roy	It's a pleasure to be here.
Host	To start things off, please tell us how you came to Seoul.
Stella	I came to South Korea to teach English here at a university five years ago. **I really had no idea what to expect**. But it was a wonderful experience. During my first year, I met Roy and we became fast friends.
Roy	That's right. I was also new to Korea at the time and newcomers tend to share similar experiences in a foreign country, so we were naturally drawn toward each other.
Host	I see. **So what is it with** life here in Seoul that made you decide to write a book?

Stella   That's a good question. I think writing a book was always in the back of my mind, but I just never got around to it.

Roy   I think it was when we both started sharing our experiences. By doing that, we started talking about some of the good and bad aspects of living as expatriates in Seoul. It became so interesting that we just couldn't ignore it any longer.

Host   I see. So what were some of those things you discussed?

Stella   When I first came to Seoul, I was surprised at how common the English language was. I mean, you can find English writing almost everywhere you turn. The sheer number of English signs in restaurants, subways and public places is really something else.

Roy   Yet, at the same time, because of the convenience of English usage, many expatriates find themselves somewhat isolated from mainstream Korean culture. Some foreigners have lived here for years and barely speak the Korean language! That really made us wonder and so we started to explore the situation more deeply.

Host   I see. There seems to be a contradiction even in the use of the English language in Seoul itself.

Stella   Exactly. That's why we called our book "A Land of Contradictions." We felt that **when it comes down to it**, Seoul is a complex society that is difficult to define.

Roy   Yeah, you just can't simply say that people living in Seoul are one way or the other. That's much too simplistic and does a disservice to the tremendous amount of diversity that takes place in Seoul.

Key Patterns

1. **I really had no idea~**
   I really had no idea what to expect.

2. **You're in for~**
   You're in for a treat today!

3. **When it comes down to~**
   When it comes down to it, Seoul is a complex society that is difficult to define.

4. **What is it with ~?**
   What is it with life here in Seoul?

1

I really had no idea _____ .   정말 잘 모르겠습니다.
I really had no idea what to expect.

'잘 모르겠다' 는 영어 표현은 도대체 몇 가지나 될까요? Well, I have no idea. 어때요? I don't know. I don't see. Well⋯. 이렇게도 사용할 수 있겠죠.

A. I have no idea~: 정말 잘 모르겠습니다.

I really had no idea what to expect.
저는 무슨 일이 생길지 전혀 몰랐습니다.
I have no idea when he will come.
그가 언제 올지 전혀 알 수 없습니다.

B. I don't know/see/understand. : 모르겠습니다.

I don't know why she left me without saying goodbye.
그녀가 왜 마지막 인사도 없이 떠나갔는지 알 수 없어.

I don't see how they can climb up Mt. Halla in winter.

나는 그들이 어떻게 겨울에 한라산을 등정했는지 이해할 수가 없단 말이지.

2

You're in for _____ . _____ 하실 준비되셨나요.

You're in for a treat today!

You are in for a treat!에서는 두 가지를 기억해야겠죠. You're in하면 초대된 사람처럼 당신이 그 자리에 어울린다는 것이고, treat의 명사로서의 뜻은 '한턱, 예기치 않은 멋진 경험' 이런 거잖아요. "여러분 잘 오셨습니다. 오늘 멋진 경험하실 준비되셨나요" 정도의 전형적인 구문입니다.

A. be in~: 속하다, 되다.

You're in. I'm out.

너는 계속해, 나는 빠질래.

B. for a treat~: 예기치 않은 멋진 경험을~

They'll treat you.

그들이 대접을 할 겁니다.

   A: I'll get lunch for you.

   점심 제가 살게요.

   B: Thank you. Then I'll get dessert.

   감사합니다. 그럼 후식은 제가요.

3

When it comes down to _____,

_____에 관한 한, _____과 관련하여

When it comes down to it, Seoul is a complex society that is difficult to define.

When it comes down to~는 "~에 관한 한, ~과 관련하여"라고 이해하면 되는 구문입니다. 표현 그대로를 번역한다면 "~에 이르게 되면"이 되겠죠. to 다음에 명사를 넣습니다.

A. When it comes down to + 명사: ~에 관한 한, ~과 관련하여

When it comes down to it, Seoul is a complex society that is difficult to define.
말하자면, 서울은 뭐라 정의 내리기 어려운 복잡한 사회인 거죠.
When it comes down to women, I definitely trust your instincts.
여자에 관한 한, 난 너의 직감을 믿는다.
I think it is a matter of willpower when it comes down to the final leg of the marathon.
마라톤 최종단계에서 가장 중요한 것은 결국 인간의 의지력이라고 저는 생각합니다.

4

What is it with _____? 그래서 _____와는 무슨 상관인데?
What is it with life here in Seoul?

What is it with~?와 What's up with~?를 함께 배워봅니다. "그래서 ~와는 무슨 상관인데" 정도로 해석하시면 됩니다. 상대방에게 의견을 묻는 유용한 표현이에요. 그런데 예를 보시는 것처럼 모르는 단어는 없는데, 뭔가 뜻이 잘 해석이 안 되는 경우가 많죠? What do you propose to do? "그래서 하고 싶은 말이 뭡니까?"라는 비슷한 문장을 하나 더 제시하면 어때요, 도움이 되십니까?

A. What is it with~?: ~랑은 무슨 관계입니까?

What is it with life here in Seoul?
그래서 서울에서 사는 것과 무슨 상관이 있습니까?
What is it with men these days?
요즈음 남자들은 왜 그래요?

B. What's up with~?: ~는 어때요?

What's up with that?
그건 무슨 상관이죠?
What's up with the weather today?
오늘 날씨는 어떨까요?

174

Alternative Expressions

1

fast friends
= close friends
= close buddies
= bosom buddies
= two peas in a pod
= chums
= as thick as thieves
= blood brothers
= sidekicks
= like brothers
= like sisters

Opposite: "fair-weather friend": a friend who is only dependable in good
times, but not in bad times.

2

always in the back of my mind
= I always had a mind to~
= I always had half a mind to~
= I had been thinking of doing it, but~
= I had been toying with the idea for some time~
= I had been playing with the idea~
= I often thought about doing~

3

get around to [do/doing] something
To have the time and opportunity to complete or finish some task or
responsibility

4

the good and bad aspects

= the advantages and disadvantages

= the pros and cons

= the pluses and minuses

= ups and downs

= upside and downside

5

When it comes down to it

= At the end of the day~

= The bottom line is that~

= Ultimately,

= In the final analysis~

= When all is said and done~

= It all boils down to~

6

does a disservice

= doesn't do justice to~

= isn't an accurate picture of~

= isn't a fair picture of~

1. **너는 너무 근시안이야.** You fail to see forest for the trees.

"너는 숲은 못 보고 나무만 보는구나"라고 이해하시면 되겠습니다. 근시안이라는 것이 가까운 것만 보고 멀리 있는 것은 못 보는 상태이고, 결국 큰 그림은 놓친 것이지요. 어른이 된다는 것은 미래를 바라보는 것인데, 예측을 하고 미리 준비하는 것, 큰 그림을 보는 것이 결국 얼마나 어려운 것인지….

- ● You fail to see the big picture.
- ● You're missing the big picture.
- ● Focusing too much on the details.
- ● Failing to see the large picture.

2. **나는 편한 사람이에요.** I'm never one to stand on ceremony.

"to stand on ceremony"를 영어로 풀어보면 "to conduct oneself in a very formal manner in following manners and courtesy"입니다. 온갖 종류의 ceremony를 생각해보세요. 결혼식, 장례식, 교회에서 혹은 그 외 많은 장소에 서 있다는 것이 결국은 상황에 맞게 상당히 정중한 태도로 행동해야 한다는 것이니 사실 좀 불편할 확률이 높겠죠. "저 편한 사람인데요"를 단순히 easy going이라고 하면 너무 쉽잖아요.

- ● I'm never one to stand on ceremony. 나는 그 불편한 사람이 아니에요.
- ● No need to stand on ceremony at my house. Please feel free to call me Bob and help yourself to some food! 저희 집에서는 불편하게 생각하지 마세요. 저를 밥이라고 부르시고, 뭐 좀 편하게 드세요.

Exercises

• Grammar Practice

Follow the directions and complete the sentence.

A. Add a preposition
1. You're _____ for a treat today!
2. Seoul: A Land _____ Contradictions
3. I have a few things kicking _____ upstairs.
4. As long as you walk me _____ the script together.
5. I came to South Korea to teach English here _____ a university five years ago.

of	at	around	through	in

B. Add a verb and complete each sentence (You may have to change the tense or form).
1. What are we _____ at here?
2. What made you decide _____ a book?
3. To _____ things off, please tell us how you came to Seoul.
4. I think _____ a book was always in the back of my mind.
5. If we haven't _____ anything done by say, the 25th, we're in serious trouble.

look	start	get	write	write

Culture Corner

• The Changing Face of Korea

For thousands of years Korea impressively maintained itself as one of the most **ethnically homogenous** countries in the world. With the rise of foreigners living and working here, however, that impressive reality is undergoing unprecedented changes.

There are currently 1.1 million **foreigners** living in South Korea. This accounts for 2.2 percent of South Korea's entire population. The thing to note is how rapidly foreigners have increased. When foreigners surpassed the one million mark back in 2007, it marked a four-fold increase in just ten years. This rapid rate is expected to result in foreigners accounting for 10 percent of the South Korean population by 2050. That's right, one out of every ten people in South Korea will be foreign!

Experts cite the fact that South Korean society has been aging rapidly while also suffering from one of the lowest birth rates in the world. As a result, the recent immigration of foreigners seems dynamic compared to the stagnant growth rate of South Korea's native population.

One group of foreigners consists of transient **English native speaker teachers** from countries such as America, Canada and other English-speaking countries. Given South Korea's powerful desire to learn English, English education in this country is a gigantic and lucrative market. Thus, many foreigners have regarded South Korea to be the country of choice given the prevalence of private institutes known as *hagweon* and the opportunities available at public schools and universities. However, since most of the academic institutions have one or two-year contracts, this population tends to come and go within a short time frame.

Another group is **foreign students**. Their number tripled in the last several years to 55,000 in 2009, accounting for 7 percent of the foreign population. Some experts project that this figure will double and that there will be 100,000 foreign students studying at Korean universities by 2010. While this will certainly have a huge impact on the foreign population in South Korea, they too are a transient, short-term group.

Much more permanent are **foreign brides** who have immigrated here. As more and more native Korean women reject the rural life in favor of the city and urban centers, South Korean men are left behind in the countryside and find it difficult to marry. As a result, there has been a recent influx of foreign brides from countries in Southeast Asia such as Vietnam, the Philippines, and elsewhere. Interracial marriages have more than doubled in less than ten years. According to an article in *The New York Times*, four out of ten women who married in rural areas were foreign-born. By 2008, about ten percent of all marriages in South Korea were interracial; of these, 70 percent involved Korean men marrying foreign women.

Of course, in such interracial marriages of convenience, there have been many social problems that have arisen due to cultural and language differences. There have been reports of abuse and divorce is unfortunately common. Even worse, many of the children from interracial marriages suffer from discrimination and bullying in schools. In 2009, the number of **interracial children** in South Korea was recorded at 107,689. Clearly, much support and services need to take place to address the urgent social issue of multiculturalism in the countryside.

The most numerous foreigner group, however, is unskilled **migrant workers**. The number of these largely unskilled migrant workers takes the lion's share of the foreign population at around 540,000. Most of these workers come from countries such as China, Southeast Asia (Vietnam, the Philippines) and South Asia. Interestingly, a large number of these migrant workers are **Joseonjok**, or ethnic Korean-Chinese (in fact, the Joseonjok comprise the largest overall group among the foreign population at 56.5 percent). Seeking low-wage jobs, many are also here illegally. The total estimated number of **illegal immigrants** is estimated to be more than 200,000. Because of their status, many migrant workers face discrimination in South Korea. Consequently, human rights and worker's rights have emerged as major issues for these people from poorer countries who fulfill a labor shortage in certain manufacturing sectors.

Clearly, South Korea is undergoing significant changes in the composition of its society. As the foreign population continues to rise, the face of Korea will continue to change and reflect growing global realities that will bring with it many complex opportunities and challenges.

Exercise Answer Key

• Lessons 1 & 2 Select the Appropriate Word   p. 22

1. quite
2. just
3. never
4. might
5. unexpectedly
6. until
7. remember

• Lessons 3 & 4 Collocation Match-Up   p. 47

1. best bet
2. wee hours
3. be willing to
4. shoot for
5. slept a wink
6. nothing to lose
7. rough night

• Lessons 5, 6 & 7 Error correction   p. 81

1. it is → is it
2. look → looks
3. for → with
4. see → seen
5. on → at
6. visiting to Seoul → visiting Seoul
7. to 삭제

• Lessons 8, 9 & 10 Match-Up Words and Meaning   p. 177

| 1. C | 3. A | 5. E | 7. F |
| 2. G | 4. B | 6. D | |

Lessons 11, 12 & 13 Crossword Puzzle   p. 152~153

Across
1. secretary
4. earnestness
5. conclusion
6. possibility
9. reliable

Down
2. candidate
3. correspondence
6. property
7. estate
8. investor

Lessons 14 & 15 Grammar Practice   p. 178

A.
1. in
2. of
3. around
4. through
5. at

B.
1. looking
2. to write
3. to start
4. writing
5. gotten

Korean Translation

소영: 얘들아! 방금 깜짝 놀랄 일이 생겼어!

제니퍼: 뭔데? 말해봐!

소영: 알렉스의 누나가 갑자기 서울에 온다는데, 그래서 이번 주말에 저녁식사를 함께 해야만 해.

제니퍼: 우와. 그래서 스트레스받은 거야?

제인: 그게 어쨌다는 거야? 그래서 그의 누나를 만난다는 거잖아. 네가 그의 부모님을 만나는 것도 아닌데 뭘.

제니퍼: 너는 이해할 수 없을 거야. 알렉스는 그의 누나와 매우 친해. 그는 정말 그녀를 존경하고 그 누구보다 그녀의 의견을 존중해. 그의 부모님을 포함해서 말이야.

제인: 어머! 마마보이보다 더 안 좋아! 그는 누나 보이(누나말만 따르는)구나!

소영: 넌 도움이 안 돼! 네가 내 입장이라면 어떻게 할 것 같아?

제인: 알았어. 알았다고. 난 그냥 농담이야. 진지하게 말해서. 최악이라고 해봤자 뭐 있겠어?

소영: 내가 좋은 첫인상을 남기지 못할까봐 걱정이야. 첫 단추를 잘 끼워야 할 텐데.

제니퍼: 내가 너라면 걱정하지 않을 것 같아. 그냥 편하게 마음을 갖고 침착해! 너희 둘은 잘 지낼 수 있을 거야.

제인: 응, 걱정마. 너의 감정을 드러내라고. 너는 괜찮을 거야. 나는 모든 것이 잘될 거라고 확신해.

소영: 내가 좀 긴장한 것 같아. 말하자면 알렉스는 그의 누나의 의견을 정말 많이 염두에 두거든. 그녀는 그의 삶에 큰 영향을 끼치고 있어. 그는 그녀의 말을 모두 다 듣거든!

제인: 음. 그건 별로 좋게 들리지 않는데. 아마도 그는 결국 네가 만나길 원하는 남자가 아닌 것 같아.

소영: 어휴, 날 좀 그만 웃길래? 난 정말 너희들의 도움이 필요하다고!

제니퍼: 소영아 우리가 있잖아. 우리가 어떻게 도와줘야 하는지 말해봐.

소영: 내가 무슨 옷을 입어야 하는지부터 말해줘!

• Lesson 2

그레이스: 좋은 시간이었어. 저녁도 맛있었고.

알렉스: 소영이와 만나줘서 고마워. 그녀 괜찮지 않아?

그레이스: 좋은 사람 같아. 그리고 난 그녀의 옷차림새가 너무 마음에 들었어. 패션을 보는 안목이 있어.

알렉스: 응. 그녀는 확실히 옷이나 음식 같은 것을 보는 데 일가견이 있는 것 같아. 그런데 그녀의 성격은 어떤 것 같아?

그레이스: 도대체 안 좋을 게 뭐 있어? 그녀는 정말 내성적인 것 같더라. 반면에 넌 매우 사교성이 좋잖아. 내 생각에 그녀는 너와 아주 잘 어울릴 것 같아. 넌 정말 그녀가 도망가지 않도록 잘 해야 돼!

알렉스: 누나가 그런 말 할 줄 알았어. 내 생각에 내가 소영이에게 누나에 관한 이야기를 너무 많이 해서 좀 긴장한 것 같았어. 내가 얼마나 누나의 의견을 존중하는지 알거든!

그레이스: 알렉스! 그러면 안 돼! 난 너의 판단을 믿어! 어쨌든, 내가 어떻게 생각하는지가 중요한 게 아냐. 정말 중요한 건 너의 생각이야.

알렉스: 하하. 나도 알아. 내가 말하고자 하는 건 내게 있어서 누나가 그녀를 만났다는 사실이 중요하다는 거야. 난 단지 누나와 그녀가 잘 지내기를 바랄 뿐이라고.

그레이스: 물론이지. 우린 잘 지낼 거야. 왜 우리가 안 그러겠어? 바보 같아. 그런데 나 정말 너에게 물어보고 싶은 것이 있어. 이 소식을 엄마와 아빠에게 언제 말씀드릴 예정이니?

알렉스: 음. 무슨 의미야?

그레이스: 모르는 척하지 말라고. 내가 무슨 말 하는지 알잖아. 결혼 말이야!

알렉스: 하하! 누나가 말하는 것에 대해 별 생각이 없는데. 너무 이른 것 같지 않아?

그레이스: 어머머! 너희들은 결혼에 대해 아직 이야기를 해보지 않았다는 거야? 너 지난 6개월간 매우 진지했잖아. 그건 최소한 화제가 됐어야 한다고.

알렉스: 누나! 여유를 좀 줘. 시간이 많이 남아 있잖아. 어머니와 아버지는 다음 달에 서울에 오신데. 그때 말씀드려볼게.

그레이스: 네가 무슨 말을 하던 간에 중요하게 기억해야 할 것은 여자가 영원히 기다려주지 않는다는 거야. 내가 너였다면 반지를 알아 봤을텐데! 넌 정말 무언가가 사라지기 전까진 그 진가를 모르는구나!

• Lesson 3

소영: 이봐요 매튜, 피곤해 보여요.

매튜: 지난밤에 거의 잠을 자지 못했어요.

소영: 밤 샜어요?

매튜: 우리 윗집 사람들 때문이에요. 덕분에 뜬눈으로 밤을 새웠다니까요. 나는 그들에게 좋게 이야기를 하려고 노력했고 심지어 집주인에게 항의를 했었지만 소용없었어요. 그들은 엄청 시끄러웠어요.

소영: 당신도 알다시피 당신은 언제나 새 아파트로 이사 갈 수 있잖아요. 그렇죠? 그게 좀 귀찮다는 건 알지만, 당신이 이렇게 행복하지 않다면서, 왜 당신 스스로를 괴롭혀요?

매튜: 네. 그래서 생각해봤어요. 그런데 문제는 어떻게 해결해야 하는지를 모른다는 거죠. 서울에서 아파트를 구하기에 좋은 곳은 어디인지 알아요?

소영: 대부분의 사람이 부동산 중개인이나 인터넷을 통해요. 내가 듣기로 부동산 중개인이 제일 좋다고 들었어요. 특히 당신 같은 외국인에게는.

매튜: 잠깐만요. 부동산 중개인이 뭐지요?

소영: 그건 real estate agent의 한국어 표현이에요. 대부분 어느 동네나 부동산 사무실이 있어요. 그리고 중개인은 수수료를 받고 일을 해요. 당신이 무엇을 필요로 하는지, 가격이나 공간 그 외 여러 가지 것들을 말하면 돼요.

매튜: 좋은데요. 제게 필요한 건 지하철에 접근하기 쉬운 조용한 방이에요. 전 그거면 만족해요.

소영: 영자신문의 안내광고를 확인해보는 것도 좋을 거예요. 제가 알기에 서울에 사는 외국인들은 때때로 판매 글을 올리거든요.

매튜: 소영 씨, 고마워요. 안내광고를 한번 확인해봐야겠어요.

거주인: 여보세요?

매튜: 여보세요. 코리아헤럴드에서 당신의 광고를 봤습니다. 저는 당신의 아파트에 관심이 있는데요. 아직 남아 있어요?

거주인: 네, 있습니다. 66평방미터의 작은 스튜디오지만 세탁기가 있고, 인터넷 연결이 되어 있습니다. 저는 한 달 정도 살았고 제 계약을 인계해주실 분이 필요해요. 제가 인계하기로 집주인과 약속했거든요.

매튜: 그러면 벽은 어떤가요? 두꺼운가요?

거주인: 어, 아마도요. 당신이 의미하는 것이 맞다면, 무척 단단한 것으로 되어 있어요.

매튜: 휴! 그거 다행이네요.

거주인: 왜 그러시는 거죠?

매튜: 당신은 저희 윗집 사람들을 믿지 못할 거에요. 벽이 종잇장 두께거든요. 맹세코 전 그들의 헛기침 소리까지 들을 수 있어요. 그들이 조용하다면 그것쯤은 괜찮은데, 그들은 새벽시간에도 파티하기를 좋아해요. 정말 환장하겠다니까요.

거주인: 오, 알겠어요. 음, 당신은 이곳 이웃들에 대해서는 그런 걱정을 안 해도 돼요. 그들은 생쥐처럼 매우 조용하거든요.

매튜: 알았어요. 지금 광고에서 보면 월세는 한 달에 65만 원이고 보증금은 1천만 원이네요. 공과금은 어떻게 되죠?

거주인: 전기세, 수도세, 가스비 같은 공과금은 각각 내셔야 돼요. 그리고 관리비가 한 달에 5만 원이에요. 그건 경비비와 전반적인 유지보수비예요.

매튜: 그건 좀 비싸네요. 저희 학원에서 보증금은 맡아주지만 월세와 같은 돈은 어떻게 될지 모르겠거든요.

거주인: 만약 당신의 학원이 보증금을 약간 더 지급하고 월세를 조금 낮춰달라고 집주인에게 이야기해보는 것은 어때요?

매튜: 저도 그랬으면 좋겠네요. 하지만 모르겠어요. 당신 생각에 그게 가능할까요?

거주인: 한번 해봐요. 그건 물어볼 가치가 있어요. 집주인은 많은 외국인 세입자를 상대하거든요. 그는 우리와 같은 상황을 잘 알 거에요. 당신의 학원은 잘 모르겠지만.

매튜: 음. 제 생각에 물어봐서 나쁠 것은 없겠네요. 만약 우리가 무언가를 협상할 수 있다면 10만 원이라도 월세를 낮추고 싶어요. 한번 조율해봐야겠네요.

메리: 곧 점심시간이 되겠네요. 우리 제일 먼저 현금을 좀 찾아봐요. 그런데 이 지도에는 정보가 없어요.

스티븐: 우리가 어디서 현금인출기를 찾을 수 있을까요? 우리 어떻게 하는 게 좋을까요?

메리: 글쎄요. 우리 계속 이러면 같은 자리만 맴돌게 될 거예요. 우리 누구한테 좀 물어보죠. 그게 시간을 훨씬 절약해줄 거예요. 오, 저기 다른 외국인이 있어요. 우리 그녀에게 물어봅시다!

스티븐: 죄송합니다만, 저희가 서울에 처음 왔는데요, 길을 잃은 것 같습니다. 혹시 현금인출기가 어디 있는지 가르쳐주실 수 있으십니까?

외국인: 물론이죠. 아무 은행이나 괜찮습니다. 보통 은행 1층에는 현금인출기가 있어요. 가장 가깝게는 저기 모퉁이 돌아선데요, 조금만 걸으시면 됩니다.

스티븐: 어느 방향으로요?

외국인: 우선 찻길을 건너세요. 그러면 은행이 보일 거예요. 파랑색, 흰색 간판입니다.

메리: 저희에게 어느 방향인지 정확히 알려주실 수 있으세요?

외국인: 물론입니다. 여기 저 도로가 보이시죠? 저쪽 방향으로 건너가시기만 하면 됩니다. 모퉁이에서 왼쪽으로 돌아서 75미터 정도 쭉 걸어가세요. 꼭 찾으실 수 있을 거예요.

메리: 정말 고맙습니다. 너무 감사드려요.

스티븐: 죄송합니다만, 제가 지금 기기 작동 중이었는데, 갑자기 이런 표시가 한국어로 나왔습니다. 현금을 인출할 수 없는 것 같고, 저는 한국어를 읽지 못합니다. 도와주시겠습니까?

은행직원: 네. 1층 로비로 가시죠, 제가 도와드리겠습니다. 신용카드 갖고 계시죠?

스티븐: 물론입니다. 여기 있습니다. 제가 외국 신용카드를 갖고 있는데 그게 원인이 아닐까요.

은행직원: 그렇군요. 종종 일어나는 일입니다. 제가 대신 카드를 삽입해보겠습니다.

스티븐: 그렇게 하세요.

은행직원: 우선 이 단추를 눌려주시겠습니까? 고객님이 외국 신용카드를 사용한다고 설명
하고 있죠. 이 단추는 고객님께 영어로 안내가 나오도록 해줍니다.

메리: 거기서부터 잘못된 것 같군요. 그럼 이제 현금을 다시 인출해볼까요?

은행직원: 비밀번호를 누르세요. [스티븐이 비밀번호 누르는 동안 은행직원은 다른 곳을 바
라본다]

은행직원: 끝나셨습니까? 지금부터는 간단합니다. 인출하고자 하는 금액을 선택하시고, "확
인"을 누르십시오. 확인이라는 겁니다. 취소하시려면 "취소"를 누르시면 됩니다.

메리: 간단하군요. 정말 감사합니다. 현금 찾는 데 너무 오래 걸렸어요. 다행이에요.

> ● Lesson 7

김 원장: 에반 씨, 안녕하세요, 제가 진료를 맡은 김 원장입니다. 진료 의자에 앉으시지요.
건강 상태가 안 좋다고 알고 있습니다. 증상이 어떻습니까?

에반: 안녕하세요, 의사 선생님. 열이 좀 높고, 목이 심하게 아파요. 그리고 너무 피곤해요.
이 피로가 어디서 왔는지 도저히 모르겠습니다. 멀쩡한 한낮에 마치 힘없이 쓰러질
것 같아요. 진통제를 먹으면서 며칠 견디었습니다만 도저히 침대에서 일어날 수가 없
었습니다.

김 원장: 증상이 좋지 않은데요. 이렇게 느끼신 게 언제부터십니까?

에반: 글쎄요, 증상이 있다가 없다가 한 것이 몇 주 된 것 같습니다. 처음 증상이 나타난
건 한 달쯤 전이고요.

김 원장: 우선 목 상태부터 점검하겠습니다. 입을 벌리고 "아~" 해보시겠어요?

에반: 아~

김 원장: 편도선염 같습니다. 좀 심한 상태고요. 좀 부어 있고, 편도선이 커져 있습니다.

에반: 아무것도 아니네요! 며칠 전 제 목 안 상태를 보셨어야 해요. 너무 부어서 저는 아무
것도 삼킬 수가 없었습니다.

김 원장: 다음번엔 이런 상태가 되기 전에 좀 일찍 오시라고 권해드리고 싶군요. 의사 만나
는 것을 미루시면, 가끔 심각한 결과가 나올 수도 있습니다.

에반: 정말이요? 의사 선생님 말씀이 맞습니다. 저는 참을 수 있는 한 참았는데, 결국은 더
나빠질 수 있다는 것을 이해하게 되었습니다.

김 원장: 바로 그 말입니다. 제가 항생제를 처방해드리겠습니다. 한 일주일 정도면 가라앉을 거예요.

에반: 그런데 의사 선생님, 제가 다음 주에 제 아내와 함께 휴가를 갈 계획이 있었습니다. 여행을 해도 괜찮을까요?

김 원장: 집에 계시면서 쉬시라고 권해드리겠습니다. 이 질병은 스트레스와 관련이 있거든요. 쉬시면서 물을 많이 마시세요.

에반: 어, 안 되는데… 정말 태국을 가려고 고대했었습니다.

김 원장: 해변가에 누워 있는 것보다, 건강이 회복되는 것을 더 걱정해야 한다고 봅니다.

• Lesson 8

멜리사: 스텔라, 정말 좋은 집에서 사시네요. 당신의 장식이 마음에 들어요. 편안하고 근사하게 꾸미는 대가군요!

스텔라: 고마워요. 몇몇 가구는 찾으러 다녀야 했지만, 결국은 잘 끝냈어요.

제이슨: 저는 아파트들을 스스로 찾아다녔어요. 제게 딱맞는 장소를 찾는 일은 정말 힘들더라고요. 어떻게 이렇게 멋진 공간을 얻으셨어요?

스텔라: 저희 대학교에서 도와줬어요. 한 가지 아쉬운 건 집주인이 애완동물을 허락하지 않는다는 거에요.

멜리사: 당신이 애완동물에 관심이 있는 줄은 몰랐어요! 당신은 고양이를 좋아해요 아니면 강아지를 좋아해요? 저는 강아지를 좋아하거든요. 저는 서울에서 강아지를 키우고 싶어요.

스텔라: 저는 고양이가 좋아요. 기르던 제 애완 고양이를 토론토에 두고 왔는데 마음이 많이 아팠어요. 설상가상으로 그 집주인은 고양이들을 내쫓기에 여념이 없는 것 같아요.

제이슨: 정말요? 왜요?

멜리사: 주차장이나 골목길에 숨어 있는 길잃은 고양이를 본 적 있어요? 서울에는 정말 많은 길냥이들이 있어요. 제가 본 아주 소수의 한국 사람들만이 그 고양이들을 애완 고양이로 입양하더라고요.

멜리사: 고양이들은 들쥐나 비둘기처럼 세균 같은 성가신 걸로 여겨지는 것 같아요.

제이슨: 재미있네요. 저는 아직 서울에 온 지 얼마 되자 않아서 잘 몰랐던 것 같습니다. 왜 그렇게 생각하는 거죠?

멜리사: 저도 잘은 모르지만, 많은 사람들이 고양이들이 비위생적이라고 생각하거나 불운하다고 여기더군요. 게다가 고양이들은 음식을 찾기 위해 쓰레기통을 뒤지고 거리에 있는 쓰레기봉지를 찢어서 쓰레기를 어질러 놓거든요. 그래서 저희 집주인은 그들을 죽이려고 독이 든 덫을 놓았어요.

제이슨: 다시 생각해보니 저는 밤에 고양이가 울부짖고 제 친구네 아파트의 주차장을 허둥대며 뛰어가는 것을 본 적이 있는 것 같아요. 하지만 제 생각에 일부 고양이들은 애완동물로 길러지잖아요.

스텔라: 물론 일부는 그렇죠. 하지만 고양이는 독립적이고 도도하다고 평판이 나 있죠. 제 생각에 그래서 여전히 한국에서는 인기를 끌지 못하는 것 같아요.

멜리사: 스텔라, 당신이 고양이를 좋아할 것이라고 생각해본 적이 없어요.

스텔라: 오, 정말요? 왜 그렇게 생각하시는데요?

멜리사: 당신은 정말 외향적이고 친근한 사람이잖아요. 개가 당신에게는 더 어울리는 것 같거든요. 개가 더 친근하잖아요. 고양이는 차갑고 비사교적이고요.

스텔라: 그건 일반적인 생각이에요. 틀림없이. 저는 고양이를 무서워하거나 좋아하지 않는 사람들을 많이 만나봤거든요. 그런데 고양이들을 한번 알면 그땐 이야기가 달라져요. 나쁜 평판에도 불구하고 고양이들은 매우 애교가 많거든요.

제이슨: 당신은 고양이들이 쓰레기 깡통들 사이를 배회하는 더러운 청소부라는 걸 알지 못했다는 거죠?

스텔라: 하하. 오히려 놀라실걸요? 고양이는 매우 깨끗한 동물이에요. 그들은 개와는 달리 스스로 털 정리를 하죠. 다듬어줄 필요가 없어요. 집을 잃고 배고플 때에만 고양이들은 더러워지죠.

제이슨: 음, 전 애완용 개도 서울에서는 별로 본 적이 없습니다. 동물과 산책하거나 데리고 나갈 충분한 공간이 없는 것 같아요.

스텔라: 맞아요. 그래서 대부분의 애완용 강아지는 작은 품종이죠. 그들은 이곳의 작은 공간에서도 살 수 있거든요. 그럼에도 불구하고 나쁜 편견에 둘러싸인 길냥이들은 불행한 거죠. 그 고양이들은 심지어 '도둑고양이'라고 불려요.

멜리사: 무슨 의미인지 알겠어요. 그래도 전 고양이는 소름끼쳐요. 전 결코 고양이들을 좋아하지 못할 거에요. 스텔라, 당신에게 고양이가 그렇게 특별한 이유는 뭐죠?

스텔라: 제 생각에 저는 그들의 독립적인 느낌을 좋아하는 것 같아요. 제게 있어서 강아지는 너무 종속적이고 위압적이거든요. 반면 고양이는 그들 스스로 돌봐죠. 제 생각에 그들은 최상의 애완동물 같아요.

멜리사: 전 동의할 수 없어요. 강아지는 껴안고 싶고, 따뜻하고 애정이 넘치거든요. 강아지들은 조건 없는 사랑을 주죠. 고양이는 너무 거만해요.

스텔라: 멜리사, 점점 더 많은 한국 사람들이 당신의 의견에 동의하는 것 같아요. 제가 요즘 만나본 많은 여성들은 그들의 매우 귀여운 강아지와 산책을 하거든요. 그들은 매우 과잉보호를 받는 것 같아요. 가끔은 보석과 염색까지 하고! 그래도 제 성향은 고양이가 더 맞나봐요.

멜리사: 음, 전 언제든 고양이보다 강아지를 선택하겠어요!

• Lesson 11

알렉스: 안녕하세요. 저는 알렉스 최입니다. 방문해주셔서 감사합니다. 당신의 이력서는 검토해보았습니다. 지금까지는 매우 좋네요. 이번에 방송통신대학교를 졸업하셨다고요?

은지: 네. 지난 겨울에 영어과 학사학위(B.A)를 받았습니다.

알렉스: 그러면 지금까지 무슨 일을 하셨습니까?

은지: 낮에는 학원에서 파트타임으로 영어 강사를 했습니다. 저녁시간엔 과외를 조금 했고요. 스케줄이 꽉 차 있어서 바빴어요.

알렉스: 전문 비서일을 해보신 경험은 없나요?

은지: 음, 여의도에 있는 작은 회사에서 파트타임 비서를 했었습니다. 근데... 아 저는...

알렉스: 네? 하던 이야기 계속 해보시겠어요?

은지: 죄송해요. 제가 조금 불안해서요. 이렇게 크고 성공한 회사에서는 일해본 적이 없거든요. 사람들이 제게 이렇게 유명한 회사를 귀찮게, 응시조차 하지 말라고 했거든요. 솔직히 말해서 기가 좀 죽네요.

알렉스: 하하, 누가 그런 소리를 하던가요? 은지 씨, 걱정하지 마세요. 당신은 저희 최종 후보자 중 하나이고 당신은 완벽한 조건을 갖췄어요. 사실, 저는 반대로 당신의 정직함이 더 좋군요. 편안하게 하세요.

은지: 감사합니다. 알렉스 씨. 전보다 더 편해졌습니다. 제가 무엇을 하든 정말 열심히 일하고 항상 최선을 다하기 위해 노력한다는 것을 알아주셨으면 좋겠어요.

알렉스: 당신은 그럴 것이라 믿어요. 그런데 영어 작문실력은 어느 정도죠? 그 자리는 영어로 굉장히 많이 써야 하고, 그래서 우리는 많은 양의 이메일과 공식적인 서신 및 각종 서신을 다룰 수 있는 사람을 찾고 있거든요.

은지: 저는 작문 실력은 꽤 자신 있습니다. 제 이력서를 보셔서 아시겠지만, 전 호주 국립대학교에서 2년 동안 공부했습니다. 제 토플 시험 성적도 꽤 높은 편이고요. 그리고 저는 일할 때 영어로 편지를 써본 경험도 많습니다.

알렉스: 음, 은지 씨 정말 대단하시네요. 저는 당신의 정직함과 성실성을 인정합니다. 당신은 정말로 저희팀에 적합할 것 같네요. 언제부터 출근할 수 있지요?

• Lesson 12

알렉스: 급한 전갈에도 불구하고 이렇게 와줘서 감사합니다. 노아 씨, 우리 여의도의 그 지대를 구입하는 새 계획안에 대해서 이야기를 해보죠. 저는 가격이 좀 떨어진 후에 그 지대를 매입하는 것으로 결정을 했습니다.

노아: 제 소견을 말씀드려도 될까요?

알렉스: 그렇게 하세요. 어떤 생각을 하고 있는지 말씀해주시죠.

노아: 알렉스 씨와 이사회가 보다 조심스럽게 접근하려고 하는 것에 대해 저는 반대합니다. 가격은 계속 상승할 겁니다. 저는 우리가 이번에 구입하지 않으면 좋은 기회를 놓치는 것이라고 말씀드리고 싶습니다.

알렉스: 가격이 최고조로 높게 형성됐고, 부동산 시장 거품이 꺼질 것이라는 각종 위험 안

내에 대해서는 어떻게 생각하십니까?

노아: 모든 여건을 감안하고도, 알렉스 씨, 너무 소극적이십니다. 저는 조만간 가격이 절대로 낮아지지 않을 것이라는 데 전적으로 동의합니다. 우리가 잘못될 리가 없어요.

알렉스: 뭔가 빠뜨리셨군요. 노아 씨. 시장이 계속 이 상태로 유지될 수는 없어요. 거품이 빠질(go bust) 가능성에 대해서는 생각해보신 적이 있습니까?

노아: 제 생각에는 부동산 가격은 늘 부정확합니다. 우리가 전적으로 이번에 모든 것을 걸어 투자를 하면 상당한 금액을 절약할 수 있을 것 같습니다.

알렉스: 이처럼 급작스럽게 결정을 내리는 것은 현명하지 못해요. 구입을 원한다면 그렇게 하세요. 그러나 저는 그 의견에 동의하는 편이 되지는 않겠습니다. 당신이 이사회에서 이 의견을 개진할 때, 저는 당신의 의견을 공식적으로 반대하겠습니다.

노아: 아니요. 전적으로 옳지 않아요. 알렉스 씨, 저는 제 분석이 옳다는 것을 당신께 확인시켜드릴 수 있습니다. 여러 차례 계산을 했고, 제 의견은 변함이 없습니다. 제 의견을 증명하기 위해서, 다시 한 번 모든 수치를 재검토하겠습니다.

알렉스: 우리 그럼 한 번 보죠.

• Lesson 13

알렉스: 라버트 씨, 도대체 여의도 부동산은 어떻게 된 겁니까? 완전히 망했어요!

라버트: 죄송합니다. 알렉스 씨. 저희 예산을 훌쩍 넘긴데다가, 가격이 폭삭 내려서 바닥을 쳤습니다. 그 부동산은 이제 가치가 없어졌어요. 후일담이긴 하지만, 노아 씨가 위험을 분산하지 않는 것은 큰 실수였습니다. 그 거래는 완전히 실패예요.

알렉스: 그렇군요. 우리는 이 엄청난 재앙을 정리하지 않을 수 없군요. 이번 일은 큰 손해를 입은 채로 남겠군요.

라버트: 저는 노아 씨가 다음 결정을 내리기 전에 이사회에 이 사실을 알릴 것으로 봅니다.

알렉스: 그렇지 않을 걸요. 저는 진심으로 노아 씨가 구입에 대한 권한이 있었을 때, 좀 조심스럽게 했으면 하고 희망했습니다만, 노아 씨는 위험 가능성을 감안하지 않았습니다.

라버트: 더욱 심각한 것은, 노아 씨는 도시의 새로운 환경 정책 문제를 전혀 고려하지 않은 것으로 알려졌습니다. 그의 예산안은 원래 예상했던 것보다 훨씬 높습니다.

알렉스: 정말 놀랍군요! 책임은 누가 집니까?

라버트: 우리 손실액을 최소화하고 다음 단계로 나가지요.

알렉스: 믿을 수 없는데요. 도대체 어느 정도의 비용이 될지 상상하실 수 있으십니까? 우리 정말 엄청난 난국에 빠졌군요.

라버트: 제 생각에는 여의도의 부지를 외부 투자가에게 되팔 가능성까지 감안해야 하지 않을까 싶습니다. 우리 외부 도움이 절실합니다. 제가 우리의 상황을 도와줄 컨설턴트를 찾아서 고용할 방안을 알아볼까요?

알렉스: 그렇게 하지 않을 까닭이 없죠. 컨설턴트에게 비용을 문의해보시고, 계약하게 하세요. 가능한 빨리 일해야 합니다. 자세한 사항은 나중에 해결하겠습니다.

• Lesson 14

테리: 뭘 찾고 계세요?

마이클: 중요한 장면에서 사용한 배경음악을 찾고 있습니다. 연극의 전반적인 분위기를 살리고, 궁극적인 성공을 위해서 그 음악들이 제일 중요합니다. 당신이 뭔가 아이디어가 있었으면 하는데요.

테리: 깜짝 놀랄 만한 아이디어가 좀 있긴 합니다. 그런데 우선 당신이 원하는 것이 어떤 것인지 알려주세요. 그러면 제가 추구해야 할 것이 어떤 것인지 좀 분명한 그림을 가질 수 있을 것 같아요.

마이클: 그러니까 우리는 1930년대 부드러운 음악 등이 필요하죠. 당신이 뭔가 클래식하고 재즈 같은 걸 시도해봤으면 합니다.

테리: 그렇게 어려울 것 같지는 않습니다. 저에게 며칠만 주시면, 잘 어울릴 만한 것을 좀 생각해보겠습니다. 얼마나 급하게 필요하신데요?

마이클: 전혀 급하지 않아요. 일주일 정도면 괜찮으시겠어요? 저에게 두세 가지 정도 준비해서 주시는 걸로 우선 시작해보죠.

테리: 문제없습니다. 마이클 씨는 좀 즉흥적이고 자유로우신 것 같군요. 마이클 씨와 제가 차근차근 작업을 한다면, 쉽게 할 수 있겠습니다.

마이클: 정확히 짚으셨습니다. 저는 좀 즉석으로 하는 연출가라 다른 사람들의 생각을 듣는 것이 좋습니다. 흐름에 맡겨보죠. 무슨 말인지 아시겠죠?

테리: 물론이죠. 최대한 늦게라면 언제까지입니까?

마이클: 예를 들어 25일경까지 아무것도 준비되지 않는다면, 그땐 심각한 문제가 생기겠죠. 늦어도 다음 달까지는 어느 정도 되게 해야겠지요.

테리: 시간은 충분하군요. 제가 이번 주말까지 연락을 드리도록 하고 계속 진행하죠.

마이클: 그럼 오늘은 여기까지 합시다. 오늘 일은 충분히 한 것 같은데요.

• Lesson 15

진행자: 여러분 안녕하십니까? "토크 서울" 시청자 여러분, 좋은 아침입니다. 여러분은 오늘을 절대 놓치지 마십시오! 오늘 쇼를 위해서 두 분의 특별한 손님을 모셨거든요. 지난 5년간 서울에서 학생들을 가르치고 계시는 영어과 교수 스텔라 킹스턴, 그리고 외국어 고등학교에서 마찬가지로 영어를 가르치고 있는 로이 박 두 분을 모셨습니다. 두 분은 "서울, 모순의 땅"이라는 책의 공동 저자십니다. 나와주셔서 감사합니다.

스텔라: 초대해주셔서 감사합니다.

로이: 여기 오게 되어서 영광입니다.

진행자: 그럼 시작하기 전에 어떻게 서울에 오시게 되셨는지 말씀해주시겠습니까?

스텔라: 저는 5년 전에 대학교에서 영어를 가르치기 위해서 한국에 왔습니다. 처음에는 어떤 일들이 일어날지 전혀 알지 못했어요. 그런데 너무 멋진 경험을 했어요. 한국에 온 첫해에 로이를 만났고, 친한 친구가 되었죠.

로이: 맞습니다. 저도 그때 한국에 처음 온 거였는데, 새로운 나라에 처음 온 사람들끼리 비슷한 경험을 나누게 되면서 자연스럽게 서로에게 끌리게 된 거죠.

진행자: 아, 그렇군요. 그런데 두 분이 어떤 계기로 책을 함께 집필하시게 되셨습니까?

스텔라: 좋은 질문입니다. 사실 저는 책을 쓰고 싶다는 생각은 늘 하고 있었는데, 정작 할 계기가 없었던 거죠.

로이: 저희가 둘이서 서로의 경험을 나누면서 시작된 것 같습니다. 그러면서 서울에서 외국인으로 산다는 것의 장점, 단점들에 대해 얘기를 한 거죠. 너무 재미있고 흥미로워서 더 이상 그 내용들을 무시할 수 없게 된 겁니다.

진행자: 네, 그럼 어떤 것들에 대해 이야기를 나누셨습니까?

스텔라: 저는 서울에 처음 왔을 때 영어를 너무 쉽게 접할 수 있어서 정말 놀랐었습니다. 무슨 말이냐 하면요, 사실 어딜 가던 영어 글자를 쉽게 볼 수 있다는 거에요. 식당, 지하철, 그리고 공공장소에서 너무 많은 수의 영어 간판들을 본다는 것이 정말 특이했어요.

로이: 물론이죠, 그런데 동시에 영어를 너무 쉽게 접한다는 편리성 때문에, 많은 외국인들은 한국 주류 문화에서 다소 동떨어져 있기도 합니다. 어떤 외국인들은 여기에 몇 년간 살면서도 한국어를 전혀 못하거든요! 정말 저희는 그 이유가 궁금했고, 그런 상황들을 좀더 깊이 살펴보기 시작했습니다.

진행자: 서울에서의 영어 사용, 그 한 가지 사실에서도 모순이 드러나는군요.

스텔라: 맞습니다. 그래서 저희가 책 제목을 "모순의 땅"이라고 지은 것이기도 한데, 우리는 말하자면, 서울이 뭐라 규정할 수 없는 복잡한 사회라고 생각합니다.

로이: 그렇죠. 서울에 사는 사람들에 대해 이렇다 저렇다 단순하게 말할 수 없습니다. 그렇게 하는 건 서울에서 일어나는 놀라울 정도의 다양성을 무시하는 너무 단순한 처사가 될 수 있겠죠.